Frank was born in Aldridge, Staffordshire in 1936. He left school at 15 and began his working life in the coal mining industry. He joined the army in 1956 and spent three years as a Seaforth Highlander, serving in Gibraltar and Germany. After he was demobbed, he returned to the mining industry, where he spent the rest of his working life. In his spare time he took up dog training and founded the Aldridge Dog Training Club in 1970. It is still going 50 years later. After moving to Rugeley in 1974, he retired from the mining industry and then moved to Spain, where he lived for 20 years. This is where he started writing his books.

TO VAL

To Pam Hirrel for her help in the computer work.

Happy Times Never
To BE FORGOTEN
FONDEST MEMORIES
All the best
VAL

Frank Aulton

MASTER OF BOUGHEY HALL

AUSTIN MACAULEY PUBLISHERS™

LONDON · CAMBRIDGE · NEW YORK · SHARJAH

A CIP catalogue record for this title is available from the British Library.

ISBN 9781398462076 (Paperback)
ISBN 9781398462083 (ePub e-book)

www.austinmacauley.com

First Published 2023
Austin Macauley Publishers Ltd®
1 Canada Square
Canary Wharf
London
E14 5AA

18th Century Staffordshire

Chapter 1

Doctor Jonathan Godwin reined his horse through the bracken. He decided to ride over the hill instead of staying on the wide cart track that traversed Etchinghill. Not that it was a shortcut to his surgery, it was such a nice day and he enjoyed the views from the hill. Below lay the fields of golden corn being harvested by the tenant farmers. Wagons and horses being loaded, and the farmers wives and children gathering the corn and stacking it. Sheaves stood in the sunshine drying out before being loaded on the carts. Jonathan had just visited one of his patients, a forester with a badly ulcerated leg. The dressing had to be changed often and that is what he had just done. No more visits for the rest of the day so he was free to do as he pleases. He had completed his medical studies and passed all his examinations to qualify as a doctor and now he was a junior partner in his father's practice.

Dr John Godwin, a respected practitioner in the Rugeley area had set up his own surgery at his home on Etching hill. Brier House was a big old stone-built house which the doctor had renovated at some expense, nestled at the foot of Etching hill was convenient for anyone seeking medical attention. The town lays just a few minutes away, not quite a town yet, more like a bustling village with its markets and horse-trading bringing trade from the surrounding areas.

Jonathan guided his horse along the track admiring the view. He had just reached the wooded area halfway up the hill when a rustling of branches off to his left drew his attention. He reined his horse and peered through the trees. He could see nothing except the lower branches of the tree inside the waist-high bracken being tugged at quite furiously. "Is anyone there?" he shouted. There was no reply but still, the branches moved. Maybe it's children playing about or perhaps a stag thrashing his antlers. Jonathan decided to investigate, tying his horse's reigns to a low branch he pushed his way through the undergrowth. He was waist-high in the ferns before he could just see the horses head thrashing up and down trying to force its reigns from the branches.

"Is anyone there?" repeated Jonathan. Still no reply, he pushed further, parting the ferns with his hands. He saw the body of a man lying on the ground, face up and covered by a dark cloak. The blood was oozing through the cloak, chest-high. "You are wounded, sir," said Jonathan kneeling down beside the man, "I can help you, I am a doctor." The man's eyes flickered a few times before opening. "So you are Jonathan, so you are." His eyes closed as he lost consciousness. Carefully, he opened the man's cloak and found himself looking down the barrel of a pistol already cocked. Carefully, he prised the pistol out of the man's hand and uncocked it. The man's breathing seemed erratic, probably due to loss of blood, thought Jonathan carefully examining the man. He made his way back to his horse to collect his medical kit. Jonathan tried to figure out who the man was; he had called him by name. A large wound dressing was applied over the hole in the man's shoulder, obviously, a bullet hole or more like a ball from a musket.

"I'm going to try and lift you onto your horse and take you to my surgery where I can treat you. Try and help me if you can." Not sure whether the man had heard, Jonathan put his arm around the man's shoulders and made an effort to lift him. With tremendous effort, Jonathan managed to get him almost in a position to mount. "Can you try and help me if you can; I need you to lift your foot so that I can get you into your saddle." He placed the man's hands on the pommel and told him to hold on whilst he lifted him. It was a struggle but Jonathan managed to help the man astride his horse. Putting his feet into the stirrup it was as much as he could do. The man slumped forward but seemed to be holding on to the horse's mane. Gently, Jonathan led the horse through the bracken to where his own horse was tethered. "I will lead your horse but try and hold on sir, it isn't far to my surgery." There was no response from the stranger but at least he didn't fall off. "Just a little further," said Jonathan as he saw the gated entrance to Briar House. His mother was busy hanging out the sheets when Jonathan called to her, "Mother, I have a wounded man here, can you open up the surgery and ask Edward to give me a hand." Edward the doctor's handyman come stable hand appeared shortly and helped Jonathan lift the stranger from his house. "Who is this, Master Jonathan?" The young doctor shrugged his shoulders.

"I don't know, I've just come across him on the hill, he's been shot and has lost a lot of blood, help me get him into the surgery, Edward, so that I can stop him bleeding to death."

The doctor's mother came into the surgery. "What have you got here, Jonathan?" Jonathan managed to lay the man down on the examining bed and had removed the man's cloak. "I need to remove his doublet and shirt, Mother. Can you and

Edward see if you can get his boots off?" Carefully, the stranger was stripped off and Jonathan removed the wound dressing. Blood was still seeping from the wound. "I think the ball or bullet is still in there," said Jonathan, "can you get some warm water and my surgical instruments." Probing carefully into the wound, he located the projectile. It had almost made contact with the collar bone. Another fraction and the man would have had a broken shoulder. Carefully, he probed and with a small amount of effort managed to get a hold of it with his tweezers. "There," said a pleased doctor holding the ball in his hand, "a musket ball." He washed the wound and managed to stop the bleeding. "I'll plug the hole and put a dressing on it, if all is well later, I will sew up the hole."

Mrs Godwin picked up the man's clothing. "I think I might give these a wash whilst he's here." Jonathan turned to his mother. "Where is father?" Mrs Godwin shook her head. "He's with Lord Fairbanks this morning and then he was calling on Lady Weston. The trouble is when he visits Lord Fairbanks they play a few games of cards, so I reckon it will be well after lunch before we see your father." Jonathan agreed that old habits die hard. His father's association with Lord Fairbanks went back a long way. Jonathan would have liked to have accompanied him and would have given him a chance to see Lady Patricia whom he adored. They had been acquaintances for some time and enjoyed each other's company. They were the same age and had a lot in common. Maybe the next time his father would ask him to join in the visit. Lord Fairbank's gout needed regular treatment.

Jonathan looked in on the stranger lying in the surgery. The man was breathing easier and it looked as if the bleeding had stopped. The man opened his eyes and looked at Jonathan. "Will I live doctor?" he whispered. "Yes sir, just rest and some of Mother's broth will put you back in the saddle in a couple of days. Mother is giving your clothes a wash. She doesn't like turning away a patient unless he's freshly dressed." Jonathan looked at the stranger. "Do I know you sir? You certainly seemed to know my name?" The stranger gave a weak smile. "It's been a long time Jonathan since we were at school together in Cannock, a long time indeed. I'm Richard Turpin." Jonathan gasped. "Of course, but you left many years ago to go and live down south, the London area wasn't it?"

"Yes, Doctor Jonathan, it was and you have managed to fulfil your ambition to be a doctor, well done old son." Whilst they talked, Mrs Godwin entered the surgery with a tray of food. "Are you well enough to sit up and enjoy lunch?" she asked.

"Richard Turpin, Mother, we were at school together in Cannock." Mrs Godwin put the tray down and helped Jonathan raise the patient into a sitting position. "Ah yes, I remember your mother at the school gates, I believe you left the area, is she well?" Richard shook his head slowly. "No I'm afraid both my parents died shortly after we moved." "I'll look in on you later, Richard, if all is well I'll put a couple of stitches in your wound," said Jonathan leaving the room. His mother placed his lunch in front of him and they both sat down at the table. "Have you any more calls today Jonathan?" asked his mother.

"No, other than any emergencies that may fall this way, like the one this morning. I'll stay and keep an eye on Richard Turpin. I want to put a couple of stitches in his wound later."

Doctor John Godwin looked at Lord Fairbanks; he was a cunning old devil with a wry smile on his face. He watched as the cards were placed down on the table. "Beat that Doctor Godwin." He laughed. The doctor placed his cards down. "I think I've just done that Lord Fairbanks." He laughed at the surprised look on his opponents face. "Blast you, Godwin, how on earth do you manage that?" The doctor scraped up the coins off the table; it was time to call it a day. "Next time maybe you will be lucky my lord. Take care of your gout and not too much walking. I'll see you next week." The doctor made his way through the great hall towards the front door where the butler was waiting with the doctor's hat and cane. "Thank you, Marston, see you next time." The butler smiled. "You won again, Doctor?"

Lady Patricia was just walking in front of the house admiring the flowers when the groom brought up the doctor's horse. "Hello, Doctor Godwin, how have you left my uncle, in a good mood I hope." The doctor smiled at the lovely young woman. "No, not today Lady Patricia, he lost again." She laughed out loud. "I will not go and see him for a while then. How is Jonathan, Doctor, I haven't seen him for quite a while. Do ask him to call on me soon, I do enjoy his company."

Bidding farewell, Doctor Godwin reined his horse along the driveway leading onto the road. He hesitated and looked at his timepiece. He had promised to call on Lady Isabella at Western Hall but the card game had taken up much of his precious time, besides it was lunchtime and he was hungry. He steered his horse through the farm gate leading into the cornfield. He waves at the farm labourers sitting eating their lunch and made his way around the edge of the field towards Etching hill.

Mrs Godwin looked up as her husband handed over the reins to Edward. "Your father has just arrived Jonathan." Dr Godwin senior greeted his family and asked his wife what was for lunch. Sitting at the table, he addressed Jonathan, "I see we have a casualty in the surgery, Jonathan. Anybody we know?" Mrs Godwin placed her husband's food on the table. "I found him on the floor with a bullet wound in his shoulder; he seemed to know me at once. Later when I questioned him, I found out we used to attend the same school in Cannock many years ago. His name is Richard Turpin."

Edward entered the room and enquired if whether or not the horses would be required again today. Jonathan said he wouldn't require him unless any emergencies cropped up.

"Lady Patricia asked about you son, said you should call in sometime; she hasn't seen you for a while."

"And how was Lord Fairbanks today?" asked Jonathan.

"Not bad but again a sore loser at cards. I had intended to call on Lady Isabella but the card game took a while. Maybe tomorrow. Perhaps you should join me Jonathan and then you could make an excuse for an early departure and call at Boughey Hall and deliver some medicine for Lord Fairbanks."

Jonathan agreed it was a good idea but only if his patient was well enough to be left. He showed his father the bullet removed from the shoulder of his patient. "A musket ball, enough to put a big hole in your body." exclaimed his father examining the lead ball. "There's a company of the King's soldiers somewhere on Cank Thorn practising their shooting, it could probably have been a stray shot that hit Mr Turpin "

Edward came in and said he had unsaddled Mr Turpin's horse and fed it some hay. Mrs Godwin said that Mr Turpin was awake and in a good mood and had thanked her for cleaning his clothing.

Jonathan said it would be a good time to stitch up the wound.

Richard Turpin looked up as Jonathan entered the surgery. "Right, I'll check the wound and stitch you up Richard," said Jonathan, "let's take a look, shall we." The dressing was removed and the bleeding had stopped. "Just a couple of stitches and you will be as good as new."

Richard Turpin expressed his gratitude to the doctor and said that he must depart early the next morning as he had business in Stafford. Jonathan assured him that a good night's rest and some good food should see him fit and well but he would put Richard's arm in a sling and advised him to rest if for a few more days. "What do you do for a living?" enquired Jonathan casually.

"I'm a courier," replied Richard.

Early next morning, Mrs Godwin laid the table and prepared breakfast. The doctors took their places at the table. Mrs Godwin entered the room with the food. "He's gone, Mr Turpin has," she said, "dressed himself and paid Edward to saddle his horse. He left some gold sovereigns on the table."

The doctors exchanged glances. "Well, he said he had important business in Stafford," said Jonathan.

Their horses saddled, the two doctors bade farewell to Mrs Godwin and made their way across the fields. "What's the matter with Lady Isabella?" asked Jonathan.

"Not a lot really, she's just a lonely old widow rattling around in that big old mansion. She sits in front of the window gazing at the river. I think one day she may throw herself in; she gets so depressed, she needs some lively company around her to cheer her up. Her servants do what they can but they are not on her level. She's a very intelligent woman."

"Are you treating her for anything or is this a courtesy visit?" asked Jonathan.

"Both really, she enjoys a good chat but when her husband passed on she became a recluse, they have no other family, no heirs to pass on the mansion to, and it's becoming a burden to her."

Western Towers stood on the banks of the River Stour; a formidable looking building. Its dark stone-work gave it a sinister look. Built a long time ago, it had been in the Western family for many years. The duke of western made his name in the early days as an army officer, commanding a large part of the king's army. Duly rewarded for his service to the king and leading the army in many battles. As with many of the nobility, rewards for service to the crown were land and a comfortable payoff, plus what they could make during their conquests. Always given titles to suit their purpose but indebted to the crown.

Lady Isabella greeted the two doctors and arranged for drinks to be taken in her lounge overlooking the river. She was well into her 70s, physically fit as far as Jonathan could see but she lacked the motivation to pursue any interests. She commented on Jonathan's appearance, saying what a handsome smartly dressed young man he was. Doctor John senior asked Lady Isabella how she had been. "Oh! I do get depressed," she replied, "rumbling around in this old house is driving me crazy."

Doctor John gazed around the room. "It's too big for you now my Lady, why don't you sell it and buy something smaller."

Lady Isabella looked at the doctor. "Because it's my home, I've lived here for many years, all my memories are here; all those wonderful years with my husband. I can remember all the lovely parties we had here, all the lovely guests we entertained. Those were the magical years, Doctor John. How can I leave all those beautiful memories behind?" Young Jonathan nodded his head in agreement. "Yes, Lady Isabella, it would be heartbreaking for you to do that but isn't there some other solution. You own swathes of land along the river. Why not have a smaller house built for yourself, something more manageable. These old houses are fine but expensive to keep and very demanding to look after." She looked at Jonathan and then his father. "Your son has his head on his shoulders, Doctor John, you have taught him well." She then turned to Jonathan. "My dear boy, where is the money coming from to build this new house? The land is tenanted out to the farmers and that income barely sustains the upkeep of Western Towers. A good idea, Doctor Jonathan but unaffordable."

Jonathan's father addressed Lady Isabella. "What happens to this place when you pass on?" She looked at the doctor and smiled. "That offers no problem to me, dear Doctor, I shall not be around to worry about it."

"I have an idea," replied the doctor, "why not sell it now but retain the top floor as your private residence."

Lady Isabella rose from her chair and walked to the large window overlooking the river. "Would you care to walk with me along the river, Doctor John? I do enjoy the views." Young Jonathan made his excuses explaining that he had another patient to call on but encouraged his father to accompany her. "Father, why don't you talk to Lady Isabella about the idea you had. I'm sure she may be interested."

Jonathan looked back as he left the old mansion, he could see his father and Lady Isabella standing by the river.

Lady Patricia was admiring the flowers around the front of the house as Jonathan rode up. A broad smile appeared as she waited for Jonathan to dismount.

"Jonathan Godwin, where have you been for the last few weeks, have you fallen out with me or what?" Jonathan smiled at her. "I do apologise, Lady Patricia, how could I ever fall out with a woman of such beauty. I have been quite busy with my patients just lately. You know that summer time is noted for being a season of agricultural accidents, plus hay fever and numerous other ailments. No Lady Patricia, you have never been out of my thoughts, both day and night. I have made a special effort today and also my father asked me to deliver some medication for your uncle."

The groom took his horse, and together, Jonathan and Lady Patricia walked the grounds. "I remember when we were younger you used to come twice a week to see me, now it's very rare I see you." She seemed hurt and Jonathan could offer no excuse. He took a deep breath. "You know your uncle isn't keen on us seeing each other, Lady Patricia." She looked straight at him. "And you can drop the lady, it was always Patricia before." They walked in silence for a while. "And what have you been doing for the last few weeks?" asked Jonathan.

"Nothing of any interest, just looking after uncle and seeing to the running of Boughey Hall; A relentless task, not much fun at all. The Hagleighs made a visit to my uncle and I had the tiresome task of entertaining the two sons Lord

Hagleigh brought with him." She stopped and turned to him. "Jonathan, why don't you visit me one evening and we can walk the grounds in the moonlight like we used to do?" Jonathan nodded his head reflecting on the years gone by when they were much younger. "Patricia, you know that your uncle would not approve of us seeing each other. He has plans for your future which doesn't include me."

She looked scorned. "Well if he thinks I'm going to marry one of the Hagleigh sons then he will be disappointed, I don't like either of them."

They sat on a bench overlooking one of the fine statues dotted around the grounds. "I can remember happier times here, Jonathan, before Mother and Father decided on that awful trip to South America never to return. They just disappeared into the Amazonian forests never to be seen again. We don't know what happened to them and we have no graves we can visit." She pulled out her handkerchief and dabbed away the tears. Jonathan reached out and held her hand. "Yes it is sad to lose someone very close to you. When your uncle lost his wife it was sad. You were close to your aunt also and now there is just the two of you, yes it is very sad indeed."

She squeezed his hand and leaned her head on his shoulder. At 21, she was the most eligible lady in the area. Many young men had tried to woo her but she showed no interest, much to the disappointment of Lord Fairbanks. Jonathan reached in his pocket for the small bottle his father had given him for Lord Fairbanks. "I must give your uncle this medication," said Jonathan, "shall we walk back to the house?" He felt her grip on his arm tighten. "Jonathan can't you stop here with me forever?" she whispered.

Lord Fairbanks greeted Doctor Godwin gracefully extending his thanks for the medication he offered Jonathan a glass of wine and spoke to him cordially about the weather, the harvesting and other Menial matters. As Jonathan mounted his horse Lady Patricia approached him from the house. She made him promise to come again soon and if possible when it was a lovely moonlit night.

Mrs Godwin steered the horse and trap into the town and found a place to tether it. Reaching for her basket, she walked down the street towards the shops. She had a list of things to purchase and browsed around making conversation with a variety of shoppers known to her. Almost everybody recognised the doctor's wife and many of the shopkeepers gave her a discount on her purchases. On her way back home, she passed two farms. She called in on the second one and purchased eggs and milk. The farmer's wife passed the time of day and asked about her family. Assuring her that all was well, Mrs Godwin enquired about the farmer who had recently had an accident. All was well she was told, thanks to the doctors' skills and medication, he was back at work harvesting the corn. As she left the farm, a horseman appeared on the horizon. Mrs Godwin waited, recognising her son's horse he pulled up and climbed into the trap, tying his horse to the rig. "What have you done with your father?" inquired his mother.

"I left him in the capable hands of Lady Isabella." said Jonathan and smiled briefly. "That poor lady needs someone to talk to; she's very lonely and gets depressed." Jonathan carried his mother's basket whilst Edward stabled the horses and parked the float. "You look pleased with yourself, Jonathan," said his mother, "what have you been doing?"

"Oh! I've been to Boughey Hall to take Lord Fairbanks his medication and I saw Lady Patricia." Mrs Godwin looked at her son. "So that's why you look so pleased with yourself, my boy but as I've told you before, nothing can come of your friendship with Lady Patricia. Her uncle is looking for someone of high status to marry her off to. Someone with wealth to keep her in all the refineries she's used to."

Jonathan's face altered, he knew only too well that what his mother was saying was right. He had no chance with Patricia.

Doctor John Godwin arrived at the surgery just in time for lunch. As they sat around, the table matters were discussed about the morning's events. He asked Jonathan if Lord Fairbanks had greeted him cordially and if Lady Patricia had seen him. He also asked if Jonathan had any more calls to make after lunch.

He answered yes to all the questions and informed his father that he would be going out again later to Armatage Priory to see Brother Thomas. "What about you?" asked Mrs Godwin. The doctor shook his head. "No my dear, I've got a plan I need to work on for Lady Isabella and Western Towers."

There was a knock on the door and Mrs Godwin got up to answer it. One of the farmhands stood there with his hand wrapped up in a blood-soaked cloth. John Godwin took the man into the surgery. He had a deep cut on his arm having slipped with the sickle whilst cutting the corn. The doctor skilfully stemmed the bleeding and stitched the wound. Mrs Godwin applied a sterile dressing and fitted over a heavy dressing to support and protect the wound. The farmhand thanked them and said his employer would pay the bill.

Brother Thomas greeted Jonathan and immediately offered him a drink of his homemade wine. "Elderberry," said the monk licking his lips.

"It's very tasty," said Jonathan, "I don't know how you do it." The monk beckoned him to a wooden bench in the garden.

"What have you been doing since I last saw you?" enquired Brother Thomas. Jonathan smiled. "Not a lot, my friend, my weeks amount to nothing exciting except I came across a wounded man on the hill and had to get him to the surgery to remove a bullet from his shoulder. He claimed someone had shot him as he rode across Cank Thorn."

The monk led Jonathan into his workshop or apothecary as he called it. Brother Thomas was the Priory's herbalist and would reveal what new potions he had made. Jonathan would listen intently to the tales Brother Thomas would tell about the different countries he had visited and about the different medicines and potions each country had to offer. He was very interested in Chinese medicines plus all the other different ways they approached various illnesses. He asked Jonathan if he would call at the glassmakers' yard and pick up some phials and vessels he had ordered. He also asked if he would give the glassmaker a package he had made up for the rashes he had caught off the glass powder. Jonathan was only too willing; it was on his way home anyway. Brother Thomas asked if there was anything he wanted himself for his practice. Jonathan thought for a moment. "Yes, have you anything for gout?" he asked, thinking of Lord Fairbanks. The monk gave him some cream and then said to advise the patient to cut down on his wine intake. He gave him a bottle of his elderberry wine. "Tell your patient this is better."

Doctor John Godwin looked at the rough drawing he had done of Western Towers. "What have you got in mind John?" asked his wife, peering over his shoulder.

"Well, I had a long talk with Lady Isabella, she doesn't want to move or have a smaller house built on the grounds of Western Towers but she does agree that the place is too big for her. I asked her to show me around the whole of the house. It is massive with lots of rooms on three floors, most of which are unused." The doctor pointed to the drawing. "I suggested that she converts the lower floor of the east wing into a smaller living area just big enough for herself and a maid. Then the rest of the house could be let out into something useful, such as an infirmary." His wife agreed that the building could serve a more useful purpose but would Lady Isabella want to sell the stately home. Doctor John shook his head, Lady Isabella had said she would donate the rest of the building to anyone who could make use of it, she wasn't bothered about selling; she would give it for nothing as long as she could spend the rest of her days there. An ideal had sprung into Doctor John's head. He would like to see it converted into an infirmary. He had thought about approaching the landed gentry of Staffordshire to buy into the property, each having a share in the business. If he could persuade enough wealthy people to invest, they and their families would be able to stay at the infirmary and have their illnesses treated. Private rooms would be available until the patients were well enough. Treatment would be free of cost except for a small donation for their medication. Doctor John hoped he could persuade the landowners to invest enough to pay for the conversions. Nursing staff would have to be trained and paid for and medicines bought. It was only a basic idea but Doctor John had had his dreams for a long time.

Doctor Jonathan listened to his father's idea and agreed it would be a good idea if the wealthy landowners could be persuaded to buy into the idea and if Lady Isabella agreed to it.

Chapter 2

Sir James Godfrey and Captain Marshall marched the army across Cank Thorn to where the ranges had been built. This is where he would train his men. The king had insisted that the army be trained in the use of new muskets as a preparation for war if the northern country of Scotland didn't conform. He had enough trouble already in the south with the French and the Spanish. Feeding these troops was a problem. The locals were made to sell their crops and other produce cheaply to the army on the king's orders. This of course didn't go well with the local inhabitants, who rebelled against it. Of course, this caused unrest and troops were sent to make sure that any unrest was soon quashed. There were many fights that broke out and this caused injuries which had to be dealt with. On market days about a dozen soldiers would be stationed in Rugeley to make sure supplies were presented to the army. Their cart would station itself in the town and the market traders would have to donate what they could, and each name would be recorded with their donations. At the end of the day, if there wasn't enough produce given, the troops would take what they wanted and they were not very gentle in their taking. Many times fights broke out and people got hurt which found Doctor John Godwin and his son a surgery full of injured people on most Friday's. "The army's bullying tactics should never be allowed," said Mrs Godwin as she dressed the head wound of one of the traders. "They are just bullies, Mrs Godwin, they don't care what they do." The trader paid for his dressing and left.

Doctor John finished the surgery and informed Jonathan that he had to call on Lord Hagleigh and then he would carry on to another house where he had been sent for. Young Jonathan said he had calls in the other direction at Wolversley Park and at a patient at Brocton Hall Manor. Both assured Mrs Godwin that they would be home for the evening meal.

Lord Hagleigh greeted the doctor into the lounge. "What seems to be the problem, my lord?" he asked as his lordship offered him a seat. "Normally you are in good health and fit as a fiddle." His lordship looked at the doctor. "It's not me, Doctor Godwin, it's my eldest son Samuel, he's not in a very good mood these days and goes berserk every time anyone tries to talk to him." Doctor John looked around. "Perhaps I should examine him," he said, is he here?" His Lordship shook his head. "No but I can tell you what the problem is. He's in love with Lord Fairbanks daughter, Lady Patricia but she will have nothing to do with him." The doctor looked at Lord Hagleigh. "Well, my lord, this is hardly a medical problem, perhaps you should encourage him to look elsewhere, Lady Patricia is a beautiful young lady with the world at her feet, she probably already has her eye on some fine gentleman," Lord Hagleigh shouted out loudly, "she has Doctor Godwin, your son Jonathan, which you know is impossible, he's no nobility, has no wealth lands or tithes, it's impossible for him to think of her. Please have words with him, doctor, discourage the relationship." The surprised doctor picked up his case and left the room. This was nothing to do with his profession. Lord Hagleigh should be having words with his son Samuel, not Doctor Godwin. The somewhat bemused doctor carried on to his next call. A large house where one of the wealthiest farmers lived. He tied up his horse and rapped on the door. Squire Brindley welcomed him in and offered him a drink, which the good doctor accepted. The squire then asked the doctor to examine his two younger children, a boy aged ten and a girl aged eight. They were both covered in red spots which were irritating them. Doctor John asked their mother to remove their clothes so that he could examine them. Both children were covered and scratched themselves repeatedly. After a thorough examination, he then examined the children's clothes. He then asked if he could see the children's bedrooms. He was shown into the rooms by the squire who looked slightly perplexed. The doctor unfolded the bedding and looked closely. Within a short time, he saw a number of fleas jumping about which he pointed to. The squire immediately called for his housemaid and bedroom staff. He exploded in anger as he pointed the offending creatures out to them. Downstairs, the doctor said the hot weather sometimes causes an infestation and can be carried in by domestic animals. A packet of flea powder would do the trick he informed the squire and could be purchased in the town at several shops. He gave Lady Brindley a packet of powder to powder the children's bodies with.

Doctor John pondered on the problem of Jonathan and Lady Patricia. He knew they were close friends and had enjoyed each other's company since they were young children and that as far as the good doctor had thought was as far as it went. Now Lord Hagleigh's outburst had awakened his imagination, was there any more to the friendship, had he missed something.

As they sat around the table for the afternoon lunch, they discussed the matters of the day.

"Fleas, anyone can get fleas," commented Mrs Godwin, "you just have to look out for them and powder." Doctor John looked at his son Jonathan, who was thumbing through some papers. "Anything interesting son," asked his father. Jonathan shook his head. "No father just the usual leaflets advertising miracle cures." Mrs Godwin cleared the table and started washing the dishes. "How was Lady Patricia last time you saw her?" Doctor John asked Jonathan. "Beautiful as ever and always a pleasure to be with," he replied, "Lord Hagleigh seems to think his son Samuel is interested in her." He watched the young doctor's face as he made the indication. Jonathan smiled and told his father that Lady Patricia didn't like the Hagleighs. "Does she have anybody in mind at all for future romance?" asked his father. Jonathan once again gave a broad smile. "I don't know father but Lady Patricia is a woman with a strong character, she will decide for herself when the time comes but at the moment she isn't interested."

Edward came in and asked if the horses could be in stables or would be needed again. Both doctors said Edward could stable them.

Doctor John said he would be working in the dispensary during the afternoon. There were some potions and other medicines he wanted to get mixed up. Jonathan asked about Lord Fairbank's. "Not much improvement I'm afraid," replied his father. Jonathan produced the bottle of elderberry wine. "Brother Thomas suggested you try it on Lord Fairbanks, it would be better than all that rich wine he drinks.

29

Brother Thomas seems to think rich wine creates health problems."

"I shall be doing my tour of the landowners next week Jonathan, do you wish to accompany me?" His son looked at him. "Is this to do with Western Towers, Father? If so, I would gladly come with you. It will be interesting to see some of their reactions. We know they don't like parting with their money."

Doctor John agreed with his son, the landed gentry are only interested in receiving not giving. "Well, Jonathan, you can get them to pay their medical bills as agreed at the end of the month, I have prepared all the paperwork. I will concentrate on getting them to buy into a medical infirmary if I can, it will be hard work."

Mrs Godwin interrupted, "you will be away for a day or two. I know you have a large area to cover, so I shall look after the surgery whilst you are away. I hope nothing serious comes in".

"You have always managed before," said Doctor John, "the locals trust you and have faith in your good nursing skills my dear. You hold the fort well."

Lord Samuel Hagleigh pulled up in front of Boughey Hall, handed his horse's reins to the stable boy and walked up to the front door. He was about to knock when the door was opened by the butler. "I saw you riding up the driveway sir," he said politely, although the expression on his face was sombre.

"I've come to see Lady Fairbanks, would you tell her I'm here," said Lord Samuel, giving the butler a sour look which showed his arrogance.

"If you will wait here, I'll see if I can find her," replied the butler closing the door behind his lordship. "Is my Lady expecting you sir?"

Lord Samuel looked at the butler. "Just tell her I'm here," he said discourteously. Lady Fairbanks appeared a few minutes later. "I wasn't expecting you, Lord Hagleigh. Is there any purpose to your visit?"A smile crossed his face. "Must there be a reason for me to call upon the most beautiful woman in the world?" he asked reaching for her outstretched hand and kissing it. Lady Patricia hesitated. "No of course not, Samuel but I do plan my days and today I'm fairly busy with my father and his accountant. It's the end of the month and accounts have to be sorted."

"You should not have to worry your pretty head about such things Patricia. Will you walk in the gardens with me? I have something to ask you, a rather personal matter." She looked at him curiously and then said, "Let me get my shawl, there is a slight breeze today."

They walked along the paths amongst the shrubs and bushes. Patricia commented on how lovely the gardens were and how she spent many moments walking in the garden. "What was it you wanted to ask me, Lord Hagleigh?" She looked at him in a strange way.

"Why must you always be so formal?" he asked. "I prefer you to call me Samuel." She laughed a little. "I don't know really, I was always taught to respect people and their positions." He crooked his arm through hers and felt a little resistance. "You know, Patricia, we have known each other casually for a long time. I would like it if we could be more than casual. I'm sure you know I'm very fond of you and I can feel myself falling in love with you. Would you be my fiancé?"

Patricia laughed a little. "Samuel, every man I get introduced to asks me that very same question at some time or other and I will give you the same answer. I love having you as a friend but I am not interested in any long-time relationship with any man. I'm still young and want to meet other people and do exciting things but I'm not ready to settle down yet. You are a handsome man and your family are wealthy, you can choose any girl you want." He looked at her with sadness showing on his face. "All except the one I want," he whispered.

"I'm not in love with you or any man Samuel. I think I will know when I am. Please accept my apologies if I have disappointed you and I appreciate you asking me but I must decline and I wish you well with your search for true love." She unhooked his am and turned to walk back along the path.

"What about Jonathan Godwin Patricia, you seem to spend a lot of time in his company." She turned and looked hard at Lord Hagleigh. "Jonathan Godwin is a very dear friend to me, we have known each other since we were children; Jonathan is the nicest person I have ever known. Our friendship is very special and no one, do you understand, no one will intervene between us. Thank you and good day, Lord Hagleigh." With that, she cut across the lawn and disappeared into the house.

Squire Brindley welcomed the doctors into his house offering drinks. He knew it was a day for medical bills to be paid and he looked at the bill Doctor John presented to him. "That's fair, Doctor, we appreciate you taking good care of us. He paid the bill willingly. Doctor John then asked if he was interested in another venture regarding health problems. Squire Brindley listened as Doctor John laid out plans for establishing a private infirmary for the landowners. He listened intently and said it was a good idea but would depend on how much had to be invested. The doctor explained that it was merely an idea at the moment but if enough of the landed gentry showed enough interest, he would hold a meeting at Western Towers and show the interested parties around and explain his plan more.

The next place to visit was a few miles further on. The doctors were preparing to leave when Lady Brindley entered the room and spoke quietly to her husband. The squire looked at the doctors. "They've just brought my daughter from school, she is ill. Can you please take a look while you're here, Doctor John?" The doctors followed the squire to the girls' bedroom where she was lying on the bed. They could see at once that she was running a temperature and her breathing seemed erratic. Doctor John sat on the bed and felt her forehead. He then looked at her eyes and then listened to her chest. He asked his son to examine the girl also. When the examination was complete, the doctors conferred and then took the squire to one side. "She is very ill," said Doctor John, "put her to bed and keep her very warm. I would also suggest you keep her isolated. I'll write a couple of things down for you to get from the herbalist in town. It seems to be a lung infection and if you mix these herbs and boil water, mix in the herbs and let her breath them in. Also keep the window open to allow fresh air in. No smoky fires in the room. I'll look in again in a couple of days."

The doctors mounted their horses and left. Jonathan was curious. "Well, Father, what did you think?" Doctor John looked at his son. "What did you think, Jonathan?"

Mrs Godwin was baking in the kitchen when a brightly-coloured wagon or caravan pulled up in front of the surgery. She answered the doorbell and addressed the gipsy woman standing there with a young child. "My child is not well, can you help please?" Mrs Godwin invited them into the surgery. She saw at a glance that the girl was ill. Her eyes were running, her nose and mouth dribbling and she was shaking. She sat the child on a chair and looked her over. The girl started coughing. "How long has she been like this?" asked Mrs Godwin.

"A few days now, she doesn't get any better." Mrs Godwin had many years of experience nursing before she met and married her doctor husband and had seen many illnesses. This wasn't a normal cold or flu-like illness, the girl was growing weaker. "I'll give you a potion to mix for your child; she must be kept in bed and given warm broth. Keep a window open for fresh air and keep a close watch on her. If she doesn't get any better, you must call the doctor. Where will you be staying?" The gipsy woman explained that they were travelling north but would rest up for a few days just out of town. The potion given to the gipsy woman was an inflammatory composition mixed by the local apothecary. Mrs Godwin hoped it would help but she still had reservations about the girl's symptoms.

Lord Fairbanks addressed his daughter, "was that one of the Hagleighs, my dear?" Patricia looked across the table. "Yes uncle, it was Lord Samuel Hagleigh. He just called to see if I was available for marriage." She gave a little giggle.

"And what did you tell him, my dear?" He looked at her; she had a broad smile on her face. "I told him I wasn't and he should look elsewhere." Lord Fairbanks banged his fist on the table making the inkstand bounce up and startling his clerk. "Goodness gracious, Patricia, he'll be one of the richest men around here one day, just what you need to keep you in a high respectful position when I pass on; the money from these farms won't keep you in luxury forever. Think of the future. Boughey Hall, which was left to your father and me by our father, is your inheritance now that your mother and father are gone. I'm your only relative and when I am gone you will be alone, Boughley Hall takes a lot of upkeep and you won't be earning enough to keep it. You need a wealthy man like Samuel Hagleigh to support you, my dear, you must think about your future."

The doctors each gave their diagnosis; Jonathan said he did not think it was just an ordinary chest infection. His father agreed with him. "We shall have to keep an eye on her, Jonathan."

Lord Handley of Handsacre was the next one to call upon. Handsacre Hall lay to the north of Rugeley, and good 40 minutes ride. He welcomed them and they were offered refreshments. Doctor John produced his bill and was paid the stated amount. Lord Hanley listened as the doctor put out his plans for a rich man's infirmary. His lordship seemed interested and asked to be kept informed.

It was late afternoon and they were getting a bit tired. "We'll treat ourselves to some lunch, Jonathan and then make our way home. There's just a couple more to call on and then we'll call it a day. The 'Roebuck Inn' took their fancy and there they ordered a venison sandwich and a pint of ale. The innkeeper enquired about their day and asked what line of business they were in. He showed great interest when he learned they were doctors. When they had finished their meal, the innkeeper came over and asked if they would look at his young son who had been ill for a couple of days. Jonathan looked at his father as they examined the boy. "Is there anyone else like this?" asked Doctor John. "Well, my wife is ill as well," replied the inn keeper. The doctors checked out the woman in the next bedroom. "This is the third one today," whispered Jonathan. The doctors talked together out of earshot of the man nursing his wife. "Could be a coincidence," said Jonathan, "maybe son but let us not take any chances." They gave the man a list of medicines he could get from the nearest apothecary and gave instructions to keep the two patients isolated, warm and to mix up the potions as instructed. Also keep the rooms well ventilated. They also suggested he cover his nose and mouth when in their presence, just as a precaution. "It is an infection of the lungs and we will be calling in again to see if there is any improvement," said Doctor John. The innkeeper refused payment for their meal and assured him that he would follow the doctor's instructions.

They completed their calls and rode at a gallop to cover the last five miles home. Mrs Godwin, still wearing her nurses' apron greeted them at the door. "It looks as if you have had a busy day, my dear," said Doctor John embracing his wife. "Well enough to keep me occupied," she remarked.

They sat down to their evening meal Doctor John casually queried his wife's day. Jonathan asked his father what he thought might be causing the chest infections. Mrs Godwin said, "that's strange, I had a patient today with a chest infection too." Alarm bells began to ring in the doctors' household.

Richard Turpin tethered his horse to the rail outside of the pub called 'The Deer Leap' and went inside. It was quite full, noisy and smoke filled. He made his way to the bar and ordered a drink. His eyes scoured the room looking for the man he was to meet. The landlord put his drink on the bar. "Looking for someone in particular?" he asked quietly. Turpin leaned over and whispered, "Jack Slade". The landlord looked at a door to his right. "In there, matey." Slade looked up as Turpin entered. "Hello Dick, me old mate, been waiting for you to show up."

Jonathan crossed over the fields to where the glassworks were. He gave the list to the person in charge saying he had called on behalf of Brother Thomas of Armatage Priory and handed over the package he had been given. The glassware was already parcelled up and Jonathan was soon on his way to the Priory. Brother Thomas embraced him and invited him to partake of a glass of his latest concoction. "What is it?" asked Jonathan, licking his lips. "Dandelion flowers," said Thomas, "what do you think of it?" Jonathan took another sip. "Delicious."

Brother Thomas showed Jonathan around his laboratory as he called it. There were flowers hanging up to dry, herbs simmering in pots and oils in jars and many other concoctions. Jonathan shook his head in amazement. "Where do you learn all this from?" he asked the monk. Brother Thomas sat down on his stool; a smile crossed his wizened face. "When I was a young boy, I was a farm labourer. As I grew older, I yearned for something more so I enrolled as a soldier boy. I spent years learning how to kill people but I got fed up with it but during my spell with the military, I travelled to far off countries like India, Spain and Asia. I met people of all nations but not always in a hostile way. In Asia, I met Chinese, and these people I found very interesting. One man I met was a monk. Brother Lin, he took me under his wing and taught me about the other side of life. Killing wasn't in his vocabulary and he turned me away from the soldiers' way of life I had fallen into. He taught me about religion of all different nations and he taught me the basics of healing. I left the military and joined up with Brother Lin who belonged to a religious order. I hadn't intended on joining them, I was just interested in what they did in their sanctuary or monastery as they called it. I was enlisted as an apprentice to Brother Lin and was taught many things about medicine. He showed me herbs and flowers that grew wild and could be made into medicines. He taught me about poisons and which plants to avoid. He also taught me about the human body. How it was constructed and how it functioned, it was the best education I ever had. Eventually, after living with them for some time, I fell into their religious belief and became a novice monk. I still worked alongside Brother Lin and our friendship lasted many years. Unfortunately, the tide of war took over and it was no longer safe for an Englishman to be in that country. Brother Lin helped me escape to Spain where I met up with another monk, Brother Sebastian. He sheltered me for a while and also taught me about medicines and the human body. When it was safe, he helped me to get back to England safely. I heard about the Brotherhood at Armatage Priory and decided to join up with them and here I've been for many years, happy and contented carrying on with my work." He refilled Jonathan's glass.

Lord Samuel Hagleigh waited at Crossman's Bridge where he had arranged to meet Jack Slade. It was dark, although a full moon illuminated the area. He was growing impatient the man should have been there by now. He looked up as horses' hooves signalled the approach of horsemen. Remaining in the shadows, he waited until they pulled up. There were two men; he had only expected one man. They dismounted and walked towards him. Lord Hadleigh recognised Jack Slade but not the other man. "Who is this?" he enquired. "My partner, just up from London, we are in partnership," Lord Hadleigh addressed Slade. "You know what I want doing. Make sure it's a permanent job. There are 50 gold sovereigns now and 50 when it is done." Slade held out his hand for the money. "And where do I find this gentleman sir? I need to know where I can find him." Lord Hadleigh pointed along the road leading into Stafford. "Lord Fairbanks residence is two miles along this road on the right called Boughey Hall. You can't miss it and the person in question will be visiting the Lady Fairbanks this evening. When he leaves at about ten o'clock, he will ride across the field towards Etching hill that will be your change. Make sure it's permanent. When it is done, and I shall want proof, then you come and collect the rest of your money." Slade looked at Turpin and nodded then asked Lord Hadleigh where they should meet him. "I live at Hadleigh Hall on the way into Rugeley. Come to the rear of the property. I shall be in the library. There will be a light on and a door open. I will be there until midnight."

Brother Thomas showed Jonathan his prize possession, a full-sized skeleton. "And don't ask me who it is or where it came from." Laughed the monk. He pointed out all the different parts and where all the important organs were. Jonathan had seen diagrams during his training but not a real skeleton. "What do you know about chest infections?" he asked. "Complicated to diagnose, what is exactly the problem. There are many things that can cause irritation in the lungs. It can be anything from dust to any kind of abrasive substance breathed in, only constant vigil to see what is happening to the patient and questioning about the environment may help but it is difficult to be exact."

"We have four children who are suffering from some sort of chest infection and they look really ill." Brother Thomas asked if any of them had travelled up from London. He went on to say there was a big problem in the cities and people were dying like flies. They have put a name to it, 'Consumption'. "I can only say perhaps someone has brought the disease north, you must isolate your patients and keep them in a well-ventilated room and protect yourself. I do believe it's contagious. I will look into it." Jonathan bade farewell to his friend and made his way home. He was looking forward to seeing Lady Patricia that evening.

Mrs Godwin didn't have to ask Jonathan where he was going that evening, she watched as he toned himself up and put on his smart clothes. There was only one place he went on an evening.

Doctor John looked up as Jonathan entered the room. "Boughey Hall is it tonight, Jonathan?" he asked.

"Yes Father, Lady Patricia and I are reading books on local history, it's very interesting."

"I shouldn't get too friendly with her, Jonathan. Her uncle is hoping she will find a nobleman and marry soon. You are not of noble birth, Jonathan, we are just ordinary people."

Jonathan looked at his father. "We are just good friends, Father. I know my place, we are just good friends, we have been since childhood." Mrs Godwin spoke sharply to Doctor Godwin, "there's no harm in being friends, John, let them be."

Lady Patricia welcomed Jonathan into the library. "I've got some interesting material for you to read, Jonathan, would you like a glass of wine?"

They sat in front of the fire reading. The door opened and Lord Fairbanks poked his head around the door. "Good evening, Doctor Godwin, has she found you something interesting to read?" Jonathan stood up and addressed Lord Fairbanks courteously. "She has, my Lord, local history. I trust you are well sir, how is your gout?" Lord Fairbanks muttered, "darn nuisance doctor, a damn nuisance." He closed the door as he left them alone with their reading. "Uncle is upset with me," said Patricia, "he said I've got to start looking for a beau, a rich man to keep me in luxury, that's all he thinks about. Fathers don't seem to think their daughters want to be in love as well." Jonathan looked at her sadly. "I wish I was rich, Patricia and a nobleman." Patricia put her hand on his. "Would you sweep me off my feet, Jonathan?" He looked at her. "Yes I would, Patricia."

Jack Slade and Dick Turpin waited outside the gates leading to Boughey Hall. The moon had risen from behind the clouds and now illuminated all around. "Shouldn't be long now," said Slade.

"Who is the gentleman concerned?" asked Turpin covering his face with his neckerchief.

"A Doctor Jonathan Godwin, he is in the way of Lord Hadleigh wooing the pretty Lady Patricia apparently. He wants the opposition eliminated permanently."

Turpin took a deep breath. He didn't know until now who the target was. His mind raced, no way was he going to see Jonathan murdered by Slade. The sound of hoof beats coming their way drew him back to his senses. "We'll wait for him over the fields," said Slade leading the way through the gate. "If we wait up there behind the hedge we can ambush him." Turpin cocked both pistols. As Jonathan made his way along the moonlight hedgerows, his mind was on Lady Patricia. Slade rode out and cut in front of Jonathan's horse. "Doctor Jonathan Godwin, are you?" He pointed his pistol at Jonathan. Turpin sat on his horse, the opposite to Slade. "Yes that's me, what can I do for you. I have no valuables on me if that's what you are after." Turpin pointed the pistol at Slade and fired, hitting him in the chest. A surprised look appeared on his face as he slumped forward dead in the saddle. He grabbed Slade's horse, pulling off his mask he looked at a very surprised Jonathan.

"Jonathan, it's me, Richard Turpin, don't be afraid you're safe." Jonathan looked at Turpin. "What's going on?" he asked. "You have an enemy who wants you dead, Jonathan; Lord Samuel Hagleigh wants you out of the way. He wants your friend, Lady Patricia." Jonathan looked at Turpin. "And he would have me killed."

Turpin spoke to Jonathan, "yes he would. Say nothing of what has happened here tonight, Jonathan but be very wary of Lord Hadleigh. I am going to see him now and leave Jack Slade on his doorstep."

"Don't get involved Richard, Lord Hadleigh is an expert swordsman, he will kill you if he gets a chance." Richard pulled out his pistols. "Only if he gets close enough, Jonathan, now be on your way. Keep silent and be very wary, I shall be

long gone from here by morning. Thanks for saving my life."
He reined his horse and with Jack Slade in tow rode off into
the night.

Jonathan stabled his horse and went into the house. All
was quiet, both Mother and Father had taken an early night.

Turpin rode through the gates leading up to Hagleigh Hall.
All was quiet. He made his way around the back to where he
could see a light in one of the rooms. He peered through the
glass door and pushed it open. He could see Lord Samuel
sitting in a chair reading a book. As the door opened, he put
the book down and stood up. Seeing Turpin standing just
inside the room he enquired, "where's Jack Slade?" Turpin
grinned broadly. "He's outside." Lord Samuel stepped
forward. "Is it done, have you killed him?" Turpin felt for his
pistol beneath his cloak. "No, I don't murder people in cold
blood, that's Jack Slade's way of doing things." Hadleigh
asked what was going on and asked for Jack Slade to come in.
Turpin grinned at Lord Hadleigh. "He can't, he's dead." Lord
Hadleigh reached for his sword. "What has happened?"
Turpin raised his pistol. "I killed him." Lord Hadleigh stepped
nearer, raising his sword, he had been tricked. Turpin fired,
putting the shot through Lord Hagleigh's hand, disarming him
and blowing away two fingers. He screamed and fell to his
knees clutching his hand. Turpin went closer. "If any harm
comes to Jonathan Godwin, I will come back and kill you."
He turned and disappeared through the door. Lord Hadleigh
raised himself up and with his good hand reached in the
drawer for his pistol. He charged through the door and fired
at Turpin who was mounted and riding away from the house.
The noise and commotion had raised the household. Servants
were running in all directions and his father and brother

rushed into the library, pistols in their hands. Immediately, they saw Samuel's bloodied hand. Lord Hadleigh senior ordered his servant to ride and get Doctor John Godwin. "Burglars father," blurted the wounded man, "I disturbed burglars, I think they've got away."

The butler entered the room through the open glass door. "Not quite, my Lord, you have managed to shoot one on his horse outside."

The noise of someone banging on the door woke Doctor John who had been fast asleep; he got out of bed and put on his robe. "What is it?" asked a sleepy Mrs Godwin.

"There's someone at the door. I'll go and see who it is at this unearthly hour."

Jonathan had also been awakened and was standing in his bedroom doorway. "What is it, Father?" John Godwin lit a lamp and opened the door. Lord Hagleigh's servant gave the doctor the message and said it was very urgent. Doctor John closed the door. "A call to Hadleigh Hall urgent, go back to bed, I'll go." Jonathan got back into bed but began to wonder if this had anything to do with the earlier incident.

Mrs Godwin got up early. Doctor John hadn't returned. She prepared breakfast, puzzled by the disturbance during the night.

Jonathan sat down for his breakfast and enquired if Father had come back yet. Mrs Godwin told him his father had not returned. "I'll have breakfast then I'll ride over to the Hagleighs and see what all the urgency was about." His mother nodded her approval. They ate their meal and Mrs Godwin started to clear away. "Here's your father now," she said peering through the window.

Jonathan greeted his father with a quizzical look on his face. "What was all the excitement about, anybody hurt?" Doctor John sat down at the table and reached for his drink. "Someone broke into Hadleigh Hall last night, probably someone trying to rob the place but they were disturbed by Samuel Hadleigh and they shot him in the hand. He's lost two of his fingers. It's too early to see if he will lose the whole hand but he managed to shoot one of them. He was dead on his horse outside the library window. The other one got away."

Sir James Godfrey looked on as Captain Marshal marched the company to the ranges. Handing over to his subaltern, he marched over to the commanding officer and saluted. "Company all ready for practise sir." The commanding officer returned the salute. "A full company today, Captain?" The officer reached for a list in his pockets. "Apart from the night guards and cooks and one man in sick bay, yes sir." The commanding officer checked the list. "The man in sick bay is not getting any better. He's been in there quite a while now, what's the matter with him?" The captain shrugged his shoulders. "Not sure sir, the doctor says flu-like symptoms and a severe chest infection." Sir James thought for a while. "If the man in sickbay isn't any better by the time the supply wagon comes, ship him back to the London Barracks, let them look after him, there's enough here for the doctor to cope with without nursing any sick." The captain saluted. "Yes sir, I'll be off to ranges now sir and get things moving down there."

Doctor John finished his breakfast. Then left the table and sat in a more comfortable chair. Mrs Godwin looked at him, he was tired. "Go back to bed, John, you've been up all night, Jonathan can look after things while you rest and I can manage the surgery." John said he would go and lie down for a couple of hours but he wanted a word with Jonathan first.

"We have to make the rounds again, Jonathan and see if the noble families want in on the infirmary business. Could you perhaps start by calling on the squire and then on some of the others, tell them that if enough are interested then a meeting will be held at Western Towers in due course." He went on to say that when he had rested he would be visiting the four sick children. Jonathan took the list his father had made and said he would start right away.

Lady Patricia sat opposite her father at the breakfast table. "What have you got to do today?" she asked.

Lord Fairbanks muttered something about his gout and then said he had to do his rounds. "As tax regulator for the crown, I have to make my report. The next few days I shall be taking the carriage and visiting the landowners and foremen to check their records and of course collecting their dues to the crown. The king likes his taxes in on time." Lady Patricia said, "Good, you're taking the carriage that will be more comfortable for you."

Jonathan began by riding out to the furthest contact and then made his way back calling on the landowners as he came to them. The majority were interested in his father's scheme but all of them wanted to know how much they were going to have to part with. Typical of the rich they wanted it to be as cheap as possible.

Doctor John had also told Jonathan that he had already spoken to Lord Hadleigh and said he was a willing participant. His main concern now was for the four girls with the chest infection. He asked Mrs Godwin where the gipsy family were camped.

Lady Brindley showed the doctor up to her daughter's bedroom. "How has she been?" queried Doctor John.

"Well, she's still very poorly but she isn't any worse than when you last saw her." The doctor examined the girl. "You must keep her warm and feed her good wholesome food like vegetable soup to keep her strength up. Keep her isolated." Lady Brindley asked the doctor what he thought it was that had made her daughter ill. The doctor said that he wasn't quite sure yet and that there were four patients so far that had been infected. "Some kind of infection is attacking the lungs. We can only keep an eye on things at the moment. The alchemist is working on some kind of preparation but it's early days and trials have to be carried out."

He made his way to the north of the town where Mrs Godwin thought the gipsy family may be camped. The man and the woman were sitting outside smoking pipes. Doctor John introduced himself and asked about the girl. "Still the same," said the woman, "she's inside if you want to see her."

The doctor examined the girl who still looked poorly. "We have done everything your missus told us to do," said the woman, "but she aint no better." Doctor John gave instruction to keep her warm and fed and to keep the caravan well-ventilated. "We can't do no more than we've been doing," said the woman, "the doors and windows are open all day, we do close them at night though when it gets chilly." The doctor looked at the wood fire. "And do you burn wood in here on that?" he enquired.

"Of course we do," said the man, "we have to keep warm." The doctor said it was important that the fumes are kept away from the daughter. He then asked where they had travelled from. "We came from London originally but that was weeks ago, we travel slowly." Doctor John asked if they had mingled with anybody during the last two or three weeks. "No, we camped in the forest for quite a while until the soldiers came along and moved us on." The doctor said it would be wise for them to stay where they were for a while and he would visit them again.

The innkeeper looked up as Jonathan walked in and ordered a sandwich and a pint of ale. "You're one of the doctors," said the innkeeper recognising him. Jonathan acknowledged asking how his daughter was. "Still the same no improvement but no worse." They both looked towards the door as Doctor John entered. "Thought I'd find you here, Jonathan. How have you been doing?"

Jonathan told his father that all the children he had visited were still sick, including the innkeeper family. "I think it would be as well to get them all together so that we can keep a closer eye on them. Brother Thomas said the nuns at the convent might be willing to help. It might be worth a visit."

The doctors checked on the innkeepers' wife and daughter. They insisted on paying their bill this time before they left. Doctor John said, "let's call in at the convent on our way home, it might be a good thing to keep all the sick together in one place." They rode up the hill leading to the 'Sisters of Mercy' convent and rang the bell. They were greeted by Sister Mary, one of the older sisters who they knew well from previous meetings. They were shown to a room which was used as an office by the Mother Superior.

"To what do we owe the pleasure," asked Mother Superior making an entrance. "It's been a while, Doctor John and Doctor Jonathan."

"Well, it's been a while since your order played a part in nursing those soldiers. How long has it been, seven or eight years past?" Mother Superior acknowledged that the time had passed quickly. She inquired as to what had brought the doctors to the convent now. Doctor Jonathan explained his concern and asked if it were possible for the nuns to keep the infected children in an isolated place for a period of observation just to be on the safe side. Mother Superior said they would be willing to help and would arrange a part of the convent for that purpose.

Chapter 3

Lord Cranmore hurried along the palace corridor leading to the king's hall where many other noblemen had gathered. "What's all this about?" he asked. "The king has decided he wants to go up north or halfway to visit Lord Fairbanks up in the shires and also to do some hunting. He also wants to see if Sir James Godfrey is training his men well with the new muskets. It's all within the same area on Cank Thorn. We have got to make all the arrangements right away."

The king wasn't in a good mood when Lord Cranmore presented himself. "Ah! Cranmore, send riders up country to various noblemen telling them I will be requiring overnight accommodation at their luxury homes. I'm on my way to Staffordshire to see my tax assessor Lord Fairbanks. I will be travelling fast and light. Arrange for a mounted bodyguard and my two new horses. We leave at first light in the morning."

Lord Cranmore made his way to his office. As commander in chief of the household guard, it was always his duty to supply a mounted guard for the king. He knew the men he would choose. Captain James Holbourne was the most trusted officer to be put in charge having escorted the king on many journeys outside the palace.

Lord Cranmore sent for the captain and asked him to prepare a mounted guard of 20 men and to be ready by first light. He made a list of noblemen on route to the shires and chose five to be contacted to provide accommodation for his highness and his entourage. He asked the captain to select two mounted couriers to send to the five noblemen straight away. The nobleman would be very proud to accommodate the king of England. A chance to show off their elegant mansions bestowed on them by the monarchy for services rendered. Those pretty young eligible daughters would be presented to him, hopefully, to be asked to attend court in the future. The chosen households would be a flurry of excitement at the thought of the king calling in on them and staying the night. The best rooms would be cleaned and the huge four-poster beds aired; a warm fire and a busty chambermaid on hand just in case. The finest food and wine would be laid out and a mounted servant sent to look out for the king's party. Everything had to be in place.

The Earl of Huntington was not pleased to hear the news that his house had been chosen. He was in the process of refurbishing a part of Huntington Lodge and the surprising visit had caused him a lot of trouble. He had to pay the workmen double pay to get the jobs done and the place cleared up ready and fit for a king. His two daughters had taken the carriage and gone to visit Lady Patricia Fairbanks at Boughey Hall so a messenger had to be sent to make sure they were back at Huntington Lodge well before the king's arrival.

Lord Fairbanks had received the message and was busy getting his paperwork and records up to date to present to his majesty on his arrival.

Lady Patricia was busy getting Boughey Hall ready for the king's visit, everything had to be just right; there was a lot to do. The Earl of Huntington's daughters had just got the message and were preparing to depart. "Make yourself extra pretty, Patricia, maybe we'll all be invited to the palace." Lady Patricia shook her head. "I don't want to leave uncle so I won't go even if I'm asked."

Doctor Jonathan asked his father if the infection could have been passed on by someone travelling up from London, it seems as if that's how it's spreading. His father said it was possible but what had made him think of that. Jonathan told him about the gipsy girl. "They travel the country and have recently arrived in Rugeley." Doctor John suggested it was possible but so had the soldiers who were training in the forest. "Well, perhaps we should pay them a visit," suggested Jonathan. "Alright, let's do it now while it's fresh in our mind," said his father.

They rode across Cank Thorn staying on the main road until they came within earshot of the musket fire. "Can't be far away now, should be sentries posted somewhere around here. They came to a barrier manned by two sentries." Doctor John introduced himself and asked if they could be taken to the commanding officer. They were led to a large clearing where the camp had been erected and handed over to another guard who told them to follow him. The commanding officer sat in his tent looking at target reports laid out on the table. The doctors stood before him and introduced themselves. Sir James listened as the doctor pointed out their concern. Doctor John asked if any of his soldiers had been taken ill. Sir James looked at them and told them only one man had reported sick and he was being treated by the camp doctor. Doctor John asked if they could see the doctor. He was immediately sent for and introduced as Lieutenant James Fitzwilliam, an eminent doctor of good standing who had been army doctor for a considerable number of years and had a good reputation. The doctors shook hands and repeated their concern asking the lieutenant about his patient. He told them that at first it was a bad case of flu but his patient wasn't responding to the usual treatment. Doctor John asked if they could see the patient. They were shown to a tent where the sick soldier lay. Lieutenant Fitzwilliam lifted the flap for the doctors to enter. They covered their nose and mouth with handkerchiefs as they looked at the patient. One look told them that this was another case but the soldier was a lot worse. They returned to the commanding officer's tent and told him of the other cases and what they had proposed to do. "We would like your soldier to be taken to the convent and be kept in isolation with the other cases as a precaution. We are not 100% sure of our findings but we are pretty sure this is a contagious disease that could be spreading. We wish to isolate the patients we have got and monitor them. We will be seeking information from other doctors before we reach our find conclusion."

The commanding officer gave his permission and gave the camp doctor instructions to have the soldier taken by cart to the convent. Doctor John also requested that the soldiers should not be allowed into the town for fear of spreading the disease. The army doctor said that it would be a good idea but for a short while only as the soldiers need some form of relaxation after being on the ranges all day.

As they rode home, Doctor John said he would be contacting a couple of eminent doctors in the area for a second opinion. He asked that Jonathan sees that the convent isolation ward is set up and then visit the patients and get them up to the convent.

Doctor John said he had to visit Lady Isabella and set up a meeting with the noblemen at Western Towers.

Early next morning, they both set off on their respective journeys, Jonathan took the carriage in case any of the patients were too weak to make it on their own. Squire Brindley agreed to take his daughter to the convent later that day. The innkeeper said he would get someone to take his son and wife to the convent. Jonathan approached the gipsy caravan. He could still hear the girl coughing. The gipsies asked if the girl could travel with the doctor if her mother could accompany her. Jonathan made his way to the convent where he was met by Mother Superior. "This way, Doctor." She directed them along corridors to the rear of the convent. "We have allocated the rear hall as an isolation ward, Doctor; the sun shines on it most of the day and blows fresh air this way from the north east. We have sectioned off six bed spaces for your patients and I have allocated three of my best nuns to look after them. Now put that girl in one of the beds but the mother cannot stay here, she must understand that and visiting times will be explained to her." Jonathan thanked Mother Superior and informed the gipsy woman of the rules regarding visiting.

It took almost a week for Doctor John to get the meeting arranged and the date was sent to all concerned.

Doctor John said to Jonathan that if the patients in the isolation ward did not improve, he would consult two other doctors in the area and ask if they would come and give a diagnosis. If it was a contagious disease, all doctors in Staffordshire would have to be notified. In the meantime, they would visit the school in town and check the children as a precaution.

Lord Cranmore was up early to see if everything was ready for the king's departure. The armed guard was waiting patiently down in the courtyard plus the king's two recently purchased horses. Captain Holbourne met Cranmore in the corridor and asked if he knew which horse the king would be riding when they set off. "Oh! Make it the bay mare," he said sharply, "God knows, he's never ridden either of them since he acquired them."

It was eight o'clock. Cranmore made his way to the king's quarters to inform his majesty that all was ready for an early start. The king, however, was more interested in one of the queen's ladies in waiting. He took her arm and disappeared into his chambers. Cranmore paced the floor amidst the tittering and raucous behaviour coming from the other side of the door. Eventually, the door opened and the lady in waiting emerged flustered and adjusting her dress. The king greeted Cranmore with a smile of contentment on his face. "Are we ready, Cranmore?" he shouted.

Doctor John arrived early at Western Towers; the meeting had been arranged for eleven o'clock. He walked into the building and met Lady Isabella being led around the hallway by her maid. On seeing Doctor John, she paused. "I shall be out of your way, Doctor, I'm just going over to the east wing." Doctor John greeted her and said he hoped the meeting goes well and proves to be fruitful.

The carriages started to arrive and parked up in front of the large building. The noblemen greet each other cordially. 12 carriages arrived and parked up. Doctor John greeted the visitors in the entrance hall. He said he was pleased that all interested parties had arrived. He began by taking them on a grand tour of Western Towers, explaining what he had planned and hoping they were all in favour. The Earl of Huntington asked Doctor John if any plans had been drawn up for them to see. The doctor said not at this stage. This was only a preliminary visit for the interested parties to view the building concerned. They were shown on all three floors and all rooms to be converted were open to them to view. The tour took three quarters of an hour, after which Doctor John led the party back down to the ground floor and into the library where drinks and chairs had been laid out. Doctor John asked the party to be seated. "My lords you have seen the place, now let's talk, are you still in favour of the idea?" The lords had been talking amongst themselves during the tour and Doctor John had been asked many questions. He had made it quite clear to all that Western Hall was being donated by Lady Isabella with only the ground floor of the east wing solely kept for her own use and privacy.

It was now up to the noblemen to invest in the redevelopment and to establish an infirmary solely for their use; Doctor John, who was still interested. "Please raise your hands if you are." Lord Fairbanks stood up and asked Doctor John how much money was being requested of them. "A fair question," answered the doctor, "of course, the more you can invest the better it will be. Remember all the alterations have to be made. Lady Isabella's ground floor residence will have to be altered the ground floor reception area to be altered and an office reception and consulting rooms installed. A dispensary will also be required, not forgetting nursing staff, cleaners and cooks that will be required. This has not been worked out yet. The first thing is to see how much will be invested by yourselves."

"Have you any recommendations?" asked Squire Brindley.

Doctor John shrugged his shoulders. "No I haven't, as much as possible but I have an idea, if your lordships will write on a piece of paper what you are willing to donate, perhaps we can reach some sort of figure." Doctor John provided pieces of paper and quills. "No names are necessary at this stage," he said. He waited for the pieces of paper to be handed back to him. "All of you have been conservative with your donations, a sum of four thousand pounds in total. I have at least a figure I can work to. I will now get estimates for everything and see if this is going to be a viable project. Another meeting will be necessary my lords when all the figures are in. I thank you for your interest and your precious time this morning."

The king and his entourage set off on their journey north. The bay mare's performance seemed to satisfy the king, he patted her frequently. They travelled at a medium pace along the North Road, stopping occasionally at isolated taverns to rest the horses and to quench their thirsts. The king never carried any money with him so it fell on Captain Holbourne to pay the bill. They travelled well and there were moments when the king would put the bay mare into a full gallop. "She moves well, Captain, I'm very pleased with her." They travelled for a further two hours and then called in at the Wayfarers Inn on the North Road where they were shown to a private room at the rear of the inn. The king was shown into a secluded alcove where his meal had been set out for him. He tucked into a rich roast and the best wine served to him by a nice looking barmaid. The captain again paid the bill. The king used the privy and was ready to move on. Where are we staying tonight, Captain?" he asked as he mounted the bay mare. "Northampton sire, at the Earl of Rugby's estate. I hear it is quite a pleasant stately home," the king muttered something but it was inaudible to the captain.

Mrs Godwin looked out of the window as their carriage pulled in. Edward greeted Jonathan and parked the carriage and then unharnessed the horse. "Have you seen your father at all, Jonathan?" He shook his head. "No Mother but he shouldn't be long now, it's way past lunchtime and he said he would be back by then but you never know some of those nobles can talk, they can keep you hanging around forever." Mrs Godwin placed his lunch on the table. "We'll start without him, I'm hungry." Jonathan asked his mother if she had been busy at all in the surgery. She shook her head. "No not really, a couple of farmhands with cuts and a mother and daughter with a suspected pregnancy. How about you? Is everything set up at the convent?" Before Jonathan could reply, the sound of horses' hooves echoed outside. "Father's here," he said.

"Whew! What a morning," said Doctor John embracing his wife, "hello Jonathan, is all well at the convent?" Jonathan assured him that everything was on hand. All the patients in the isolation ward are being cared by the nuns.

Brother Thomas looked up as the young doctor entered his herb garden. "Jonathan, please take a seat. I want you to try something, a new recipe of mine." The monk reached for a jar off the shelf inside his apothecary and sat beside Jonathan. He opened up the jar to reveal a paste-like substance which he held up for Jonathan to sniff. "Whew what's that?" the doctor asked.

"It's eucalyptus tree." Jonathan took another sniff. "What's it for?" he asked.

Brother Thomas explained that he had received a shipment of herbs from his contact in China and had been instructed to make a paste from this particular herb. "Rub it on your chest and breathe in," said the excited monk. Jonathan did and said it had a powerful smell and also a warming effect. Brother Thomas said he had tried it out on some of the novices who had complained about sore throats and colds and it had helped them. "Why don't you try it on your patients with the lung infection, who knows it may help."

At the convent, early morning prayers were said for the patients before they were allowed to wash and tend to ablutions. Their beds were made fresh and breakfast was served at their bedside. All patients were then put back into bed and wrapped up warm. Potions were administered and the windows of the isolation ward fully opened to the morning air no matter what the weather. Jonathan visited each patient carefully making notes on their progress if any. The soldier was kept at the end of the ward screened off from the rest. Jonathan spoke to him and asked how he was. He told the doctor he appreciated being brought to the convent and said he felt a lot more comfortable but he was still coughing and had difficulty breathing normally. Jonathan took the paste that Brother Thomas had made and showed it to the soldier saying it was a new preparation and would he be willing to try it out. The soldier said he would try anything. Jonathan said he had tried it himself and felt it to be very warming and beneficial.

The nun said she would apply the paste as directed and monitor the patient.

Brother Thomas greeted the doctor and poured a drink from a bottle on the table. "What is this one?" asked Jonathan.

"It is rosehip, a kind of syrup I have made up. I made it up from an old recipe I came across on my travels. Mixed with a glass of warm water and a spoonful of honey it makes a nice drink and beneficial to the sick."

The monk picked up a bunch of the sticks which he was trimming down and placing in a container of liquid. "What's that?" asked a curious Jonathan. "Another little remedy from the Orient, they called them joss sticks." Jonathan watched as his friend held one over a candle…it began to burn slowly and then just to smoulder. Brother Thomas stuck it into a lump of clay on the table and watched it burn. "Smells like lavender," said Jonathan as the smoke from the burning stick began to float around the room. "That's exactly what this one is but there are numerous smells that can be created from different herbs and flowers. All harmless but it makes the air fresher and gets rid of unwanted smells. Take some Jonathan and try them in your surgery."

Mrs Godwin was cleaning around in the surgery when Jonathan walked in. "How are things at the convent?" she asked. Jonathan said that all the patients were comfortable. "Any improvement?" she asked. Jonathan said none that he had noticed but said the nuns were doing a good job of taking care of them. "It's early days yet," he added.

He lit one of the sticks and placed it on the window ledge in a small bottle. "I can smell something burning," said Mrs Godwin, looking around the surgery. Jonathan smiled and pointed towards the stick producing a wisp of smoke.

"Another idea from Brother Thomas," he said with a huge smile.

Doctor John walked through the front door and removed his coat before entering the dining room. Smiling at his wife and Jonathan, he said, "I can smell lavender, who's been cleaning?" Jonathan laughed and Mrs Godwin also giggled. "Another invention from Brother Thomas," mused Jonathan, "but it does smell nice, doesn't it?"

While they sat around the table eating lunch, Jonathan asked how his father had got on with the architects who were drawing up the plans for Western Hall. Doctor John gave a huge sigh. "I don't think there will be much money left after everything has been done. We will have to find a way of raising more funds, I shall know more next week."

Mrs Godwin said, "Well, our little surgery doesn't earn enough for us to donate anything, does it?" Doctor John shook his head sadly. "It's not going to be up to us. It's the landed gentry and rich nobles who are going to cough up more money, it's for their benefit. I shall be seeing Lord Fairbanks tomorrow. I'll have a quiet word with him; he carries a lot of weight amongst his fellow men."

"How far are we from Staffordshire, Captain?" asked the king as they mounted their horses.

"About 40 miles, I think," answered the Captain.

"Can we do it in a day?" came the next question.

Captain Holbourne had never made this journey before so it was a guess. His military life had been spent fighting wars in France and Spain.

"I would think two days should do it in comfort, sire. I don't think the horses are up to a long stretch like that. It would be better if we didn't push them too hard. Besides that, your majesty will be sleeping in a nice castle in Tamworth this evening." They kept on the North Road or the Roman Road as it was sometimes referred to. The king had changed horses and was now riding the chestnut mare. He commented that the bay mare was easier to handle.

Mrs Godwin and Jonathan tended the surgery whilst Doctor John was scanning over some drawings and reports from the architect. "We will need nurses and other staff if this idea takes off, where do we get them from?" Mrs Godwin looked at her husband. "Well for a start, we can advertise in the town and I could give them some basic training before it takes off." Doctor John agreed that it would be a start. "I'll leave that to you to sort out, my dear, if you want to get involved."

At lunch, they sat around the table. The surgery had been fairly busy that morning so no more had been said of the matter. Doctor John said he was going to arrange a second meeting with the nobles and show them the plans that had been drawn up. Jonathan said he would visit the convent and see how the patients were doing. "Don't forget to cover up Jonathan," his mother said.

Doctor John paid an unexpected visit to Lord Hagleigh and find out if Samuel had come to terms with losing two fingers off his sword arm. He had been a good swordsman feared by many but now a shadow of his former self, angry and moody and plying himself with a drink. Doctor Godwin was shown into the drawing room where the young Lord Samuel was sitting. "Good morning, my Lord, I've come to take a look at your hand, shall we remove the dressing?" Lord Samuel looked at the doctor. "I didn't send for you Godwin." The doctor ignored the remark and sat on a chair in front of his lordship. The hand was held out unwillingly as Lord Samuel downed another drink. Doctor John examined the wound and commented on how the stitches had knitted well. He asked Lord Samuel to try moving his remaining fingers. "There is some movement, my lord, I think with some gentle exercise and manipulation you may be able to use your hand again." Lord Samuel looked at the doctor. "Use it what for, to stroke the dog, my sword hand is ruined." Doctor John bandaged the hand but left the remaining fingers exposed. "My lord, you must try using what you have left, it could have been a lot worse."

The king and his entourage left Tamworth Castle after a good night's rest and food in their bellies. "We should be there by noon, your majesty," said Captain Holbourne, noticing that the king had swapped horses again.

"We call in at the ranges and see what Godfrey has accomplished with the new muskets," said the king, "and then on to Lord Fairbanks at Boughey Hall. I haven't been up here since we used to come hunting a few years ago."

"Some nice stags on Cank Thorn," Captain Holbourne commented that it was before his time at the palace.

Jonathan picked up his bag and bade his mother farewell. He was off to the wood foresters' cottage on Cank Thorne to check on his ulcerated leg. He kept on the road leading through the forest steering clear of the ranges, he could hear the shooting in the distance. He was greeted at the cottage by the forester and his wife and a drink was placed in front of him. The leg was improving but further dressing would be needed. Jonathan asked if the rest of the family were alright. He was assured that all was well. The children were at the school which was a two-mile walk but Slitting Mill was closer than Rugeley. Jonathan checked his timepiece, almost time for lunch and maybe a late afternoon visit to Boughey Hall to visit Patricia.

The king was greeted ceremoniously by his commanding officer at the ranges. "How goes it, Sir James, are they better than the old ones?" The king inspected the guard of honour prepared for his fleeting visit. "Your Majesty will be pleased, I'm sure. Would you like to see for yourself, sire? I have a platoon loaded and ready to give you a demonstration." The king said he would and followed Sir James down a well-trodden track to where the soldiers were waiting with their new weapons primed and loaded. The commanding officer and the king stood on a small observation platform and watched as Captain Marshall arranged the demonstration. The platoon fired and when the targets displayed the results the king applauded. Another volley was fired and again the king applauded. "Well done, Sir James, you certainly have done us proud. Our army is now well equipped to keep the northerners at bay. Good work, tell our men how pleased I am and give your men an extra day off."

As they returned to the camp, the king asked Sir James where the deer were located. The CO said they were on the other side of the forest road. The gunfire kept them away from the camp. The king then asked if there were any stags about. Again, Sir James remarked that they were also on the other side not far from the herd.

The king beckoned Captain Holbourne. "I asked for two spears to be brought along, were my orders obeyed?" The captain said they had been included. "Fine," said the king, "let us see if we can find us a stag to hunt, it will be a gift for Lord Fairbanks."

Chapter 4

The king and his entourage crossed over the forest road and followed a narrow path into the other part of the forest where the deer had been seen. The king was riding the bay mare and was carrying a spear. They made their way deeper into the forest looking for signs. The king said the soldiers were making too much noise so ordered them to fall back and follow at a distance. Captain Holbourne followed closely behind the king. It was more than his life was worth to leave the sovereign's side, especially in unknown territory. Walking his horse slowly the king looked and listened. The path had opened up now and more easily to ride along.

Jonathan reined his horse back into the forest and onto a reasonably wide tract that would lead onto the forest road. In the distance, he could hear the musket fire coming from the ranges. He followed the track and saw that a young silver birch had been blown down and was lying across the track. He could see that it was possible to ride around it and steered his horse to do so. All at once, he heard the thunder of hooves heading in his direction. Not wanting to get in the way he urged his horse up a slight bank well off the track. Suddenly, a stag came into view racing along the track. It jumped over the fallen tree and disappeared. The galloping horse suddenly appeared giving chase. It's a rider brandishing a spear, urging the horse to jump the tree. The horse reared up refusing to jump and fell backwards crushing its rider. Jonathan was completely taken by surprise; the horse trying to get up was rolling over its rider. Jonathan jumped off his horse and ran down towards the horse and rider. The horse managed to get to its feet but the rider lay completely still. Jonathan knelt down beside the still form. He was about to examine the body when another horse galloped into view. A soldier jumped off and drew his sword pointing it at Jonathan's throat. "Stand back sir or I will run you through." Jonathan looked at the soldier in dismay. "This man has just had a very bad accident, including his horse rolling over him. He must be very badly injured, possibly dead. I am a doctor, sir, let me try and help him." The captain looked at Jonathan, confusion showing on his face. "What do you mean an accident?" Jonathan pointed towards the fallen tree. "The man tried to make his horse jump that tree. He was chasing a stag and the horse refused, rearing up and falling backwards onto the man, crushing him. I am a doctor, sir, let me see how badly he is hurt or if he is still alive."

The rest of the king's guard had arrived and had surrounded Jonathan all with drawn swords pointing at him. The captain ordered a soldier to get the frightened horse out of the way. He then knelt down beside the king, his wig and his hat lay nearby. "You say you are a doctor sir, then tell me is he still alive?" Jonathan knelt down and checked if the man was breathing. He examined the position he was lying in and the way his head was lying to one side. He pointed out to the man's leg which was lying at an unusual angle. "He is still breathing but barely. His leg is broken and possibly his neck. I can't tell if his back is broken but it doesn't look good. He is unconscious and probably has a concussion. That's as much as I can tell from this quick examination. My surgery is a few minutes from here, we must try and get this man there as soon as possible but it's going to be very difficult and it's going to start raining soon so it's a matter of urgency."

The captain seemed flustered and confused with the king lying in the bracken unconscious was more than he had anticipated. "We are on our way to Boughey Hall, how far away is that from here?" Jonathan looked at him. "Five miles sir but you're not going to get this man there, his life is in danger, believe me, let's get him to my surgery as quickly as possible." The captain looked around at his men and told them to sheath their swords. "How are we going to move him?" asked a nervous captain. Jonathan looked around him. "We must make a litter; get your men to cut down two of these saplings, at least eight feet long." Doctor Jonathan kept checking the man's breathing, it was becoming erratic. "Now place those two saplings on the ground and we shall need at least three of your soldiers' tunics to be placed over the saplings and buttoned up. Now we must gently roll the man over on this side and place the litter under him and then gently roll him back. Captain, you support him from the waist down and I will support him from the neck. Be very careful or we could kill him. Now we must lift the litter. Put a strong man on each corner and when I say lift gently, keep it taught, do not let it sag." Jonathan placed two rolled up neckerchiefs under the man's neck to try and keep it still. "Right, lift and follow me." Jonathan led the party along the path onto the forest road and let them to the surgery. He ran ahead and called his mother to open up the double doors into the surgery. "Mother, we have a very injured man here, possibly a broken neck and back, definitely a broken leg." The litter was carried into the surgery. Jonathan pointed to the long solid table used for examining patients. "We need to put him on there for examination," he said to the captain. Gently, the litter was laid on the table. Mrs Godwin began loosening the man's clothing, just as her husband arrived. "What have we got here?" he asked, taking off his coat and rolling up his sleeves. "Possible broken neck and back," said Jonathan, "but we have not had a chance to make a proper examination.

Captain Holbourne introduced himself and then asked for everyone's attention. "This man, as you keep referring him to is,"–he took a deep breath–"your sovereign, the King of England." The room went deadly quiet and then deep gasps of surprise.

"I didn't know that," said Jonathan.

"No, well of course, you didn't," said the captain, "and this must be kept secret, do you understand, no one must hear of this."

Lord Fairbank entered the room; a look of horror crossed his face when he saw the man lying on the table. "Is he dead?" he asked.

Jonathan shook his head. "No, my lord but he is in a very delicate condition, we haven't yet ascertained what injuries have been sustained."

"I have sent for the doctor from the ranges," said the captain, "let him be the one who will be held responsible for the king. After all, he is in the king's service and I have also sent messages to London to bring his majesty's personal doctors up here post haste."

Doctor John checked the king's breathing. "We should at least remove his clothing and his boots, that leg needs to be straightened right away." The captain said they would wait for the army doctor. Mrs Godwin provided a chair for Lord Fairbanks to sit on. Doctor John said that it was in the king's interest for him to be kept sedated. Jonathan agreed. His mother had left the room and returned with hot drinks for everyone.

The captain kept looking out of the window and then at the king. "He's very concussed," said Jonathan, "he'll be unconscious for quite a while." His father pointed to the king's leg. "We should pull that straight now or it will be too late to save it." The captain looked at them. "Wait a little while longer until Lt Fitzwilliam and Sir James Godfrey arrived to assume responsibility," said a nervous captain.

When Sir James arrived the captain informed him of the crisis. Lt Fitzwilliam immediately went over to the king and looked at him. "His breathing is erratic," exclaimed Doctor John.

"How long has he been unconscious?" asked Lt Fitzwilliam.

"Almost one hour since the accident happened," said Jonathan, "he needs to be made more comfortable, can we remove the litter?" He ordered his orderlies to examine the position of the king without moving him. "I think it is possible," said one orderly. The lieutenant checked the position of the neck and the leg. "We must support the body and then gently roll the king over so that the litter can be removed. It is a delicate manoeuvre, you could make things worse," said Doctor John, "we don't know how bad he is injured." The lieutenant said that they would be very careful. Gently, the king was rolled over enough for the litter to be removed. "Right now we can straighten that leg and put on a splint." Doctor John checked the king's breathing. Mrs Godwin leaned over and moistened his lips. "I think it would be better if his majesty remained unconscious a little longer," said Doctor John to the lieutenant who nodded his head in approval. "I think we need to remove his clothing and try and carry out further examinations and perhaps straighten the leg out whilst he remains unconscious." Doctor John agreed and asked if the king's clothing was available, if not, he would provide a gown for the king. The lieutenant's orderlies began to remove the king's clothing under his supervision. It was necessary to cut away most of it to avoid moving the king. Captain Holbourne said that two riders had been sent to London. They had been instructed to ride overnight and notify the king's personal doctors at the palace with instructions for them to come to the king's assistance at once. "But that will take days," replied Sir Godfrey, "we must try to do something now, he will be in great pain when he comes around." Doctor John agreed and suggested a neck collar to start off with. "We don't want him moving around before we find out how bad his injuries are, so let's do that first and then see to the leg." The orderlies had almost stripped the king naked. A gown was provided but it was found that the king had messed himself and had to be cleaned. Lord Fairbanks spoke to Sir Godfrey, saying when the king could be moved it would be better for all concerned if he was removed to more comfortable surroundings at Boughey Hall. Sir Godfrey agreed.

The doctors worked together with Mrs Godwin's assistance they gently pulled the leg back into position and applied splints. "We must try and give him something for the pain. I have laudanum," said Doctor John.

"He could remain like this for days," said Lt Fitzwilliam, "the swelling on his neck and back are severe. We need to keep him rigid until further examinations can be carried out."

Sir Godfrey looked at the king. "If we try and move him now, it could prove fatal, is it possible to keep him here under surveillance until his own doctors can see him, then they can decide and take on the responsibility."

Doctor John said it could be arranged, the table was sturdy and well padded. He would make sure the king didn't roll off and of course, there would be someone watching over him day and night and he could be fed liquids to sustain him. Lord Fairbanks said that would be the best thing and he would go home and prepare a room for when the king could be moved. Captain Holbourne said that he would be held responsible if anything happened to the king. Sir Godfrey said it was the king's own decision to go stag hunting and he would bear witness on the captain's behalf. In the meantime, a company of soldiers from the ranges would be marched over to guard the king. Lord Fairbanks decided to leave and make arrangements at Boughey Hall, saying he would return the next day. Sir Godfrey said if the doctor could accommodate him he would stay the night. Jonathan and the lieutenant said they would remain and keep vigil being relieved by the two orderlies after a few hours.

It was a very worrying night; hardly any sleep was had by anyone. Captain Holbourne was very worried. "What if the king dies?" was all he could think of.

Doctor John and Mrs Godwin relieved the two orderlies during the early morning hours. The king was still unconscious. Mrs Godwin moistened his lips and Doctor John checked his breathing.

Lady Patricia greeted her uncle on his return. "What was all the fuss about uncle?" she inquired. Lord Fairbanks led his niece into his office. "There's been a serious accident, the king's horse reared up and rolled on him, and he's in a critical condition. He's unconscious and being looked after by Doctor John at his surgery until the king's physicians arrive from London to take over." Lady Patricia gasped. "Oh dear, he was supposed to be calling on us uncle." Lord Fairbanks embraced his niece. "Yes, my dear but now we have to provide a room for his stay if he cannot be moved to London, can you help organise things?" Lord Fairbanks called for his staff to attend a meeting in the library. He explained the situation and instructed them to keep it all hush-hush, no one must reveal anything.

Mrs Godwin prepared food for her guests and instructed Edward to see what he could rustle up for the king's guard, who had bedded down in the stable and coach house. Edward managed porridge and toasted bread for breakfast but told Mrs Godwin lunch would not be possible. It was suggested that they be split into two parties, each taking it in turn to ride to the nearest tavern. Captain Holbourne agreed to this and offered to pay the bill on behalf of the king. Doctor John sat down with Sir Godfrey and ate breakfast while Jonathan and the Lieutenant watched over the king. Captain Holbourne said he wasn't hungry but Mrs Godwin made him sit and eat some toasted bread. Captain Holbourne said he would send riders out to meet the coach from London who should be well on their way now. He was very anxious to hand over the responsibility to the king's physician. It had been a sleepless night for him.

The coach from London arrived mid-afternoon, the horses were well lathered after a speedy journey. The four royal physicians hurried into the surgery, their bleary eyes reflecting a sleepless journey from London. They immediately went over to where the king lay. "What happened?" asked Lord Percival. Captain Holbourne related the king's desire to hunt a stag and then called Doctor Jonathan to give his account. He asked how they had managed to move the king to the surgery. Lord Hastings asked if the doctors had examined the king and what was their diagnosis. The doctors all confirmed that a proper diagnosis had not been confirmed as they didn't want to risk moving the king in case of causing further injury the king's physicians decided that they would conduct a proper examination that evening after they had rested and eaten. They would discuss the situation between themselves.

Doctor John asked Jonathan if he would visit the convent and see how the patients were doing. He would stay with the king's physicians and see to their demands. Sir Godfrey would return to his soldiers and arrange a guard for the king.

Jonathan was greeted by Mother Superior at the convent and accompanied him to the isolation ward. "They seem to be comfortable enough, Doctor, and my nuns seem to think they are pretty stable. The fresh air seems to be helping and of course, the good food we are giving them." Doctor Jonathan visited each patient. It was true what the nuns were saying, the patients weren't getting any worse and when he looked in on the soldier, he could see an improvement. He asked the nun to apply the paste again and to administer some of the rosehip syrup and also to light one of the sticks and let it waft around the room. Jonathan felt that Brother Thomas's concoctions were helping the soldier. If this was beneficial, he would try it out on the other patients. He left the convent and made his way to Boughey hall. He wanted to find out how Lord Fairbanks was doing and of course, to see Lady Patricia. He was shown into the drawing room where Lord Fairbanks was administering instructions to the staff. "How is the king, Doctor Jonathan?" he asked immediately as he saw the doctor.

"He is still unconscious but his breathing is a little better. His physicians have been with him through the night, keeping a watchful eye on him. I don't think they have decided yet what to do."

Lord Fairbanks dismissed his staff after giving further orders. "Well, we've sorted out a room here for the king whenever they decide to move him. Tell his doctors all is ready here."

Lady Patricia entered the room greeting Jonathan warmly. "You've been very busy, I hear," she whispered moving up close to Jonathan, "I wondered why I hadn't seen you."

Jonathan greeted her courteously in front of her uncle. "Yes, as you know our special visit is our main concern at the moment and if his physicians decide to move him to Boughey Hall, you too will find yourself very busy."

Lord Fairbanks suggested Lady Patricia showed Doctor Jonathan to the king's room. "See if it meets with his approval."

She willingly led Jonathan down the hall to the staircase. He followed her breathing in her perfume. In the large bedroom, she moved closer to Jonathan. They were alone. "I missed you, Jonathan," she said, putting her arms around his neck, her lips searching for his. He gave her a quick peck and pulled away, a hurt look in his eyes. "You shouldn't do that," he said quietly.

The king's physicians gathered at the bedside trying to decide whether they should wake him up. Doctor John spoke to Lt Fitzwilliam saying he thought it would be better to leave his majesty unconscious a little longer and give the swelling more chance to go down. If they wake the king up too soon and he decides to try and move it could be fatal. After all, they didn't know for sure whether anything was broken. Lt Fitzwilliam agreed and moved over to confer with Lord Percival and Lord Hastings. He suggested trying to move the king slightly to be able to gently probe his spine and to put hot and cold compresses on the affected areas to try and help reduce the swelling. When the swelling had gone down they would be able to roll the king over on his side and inspect visually. It was agreed that the king should be allowed to lie a little longer before anything was attempted. Painkilling drugs would be fed through his mouth with the water Mrs Godwin administered to keep his mouth moist.

Jonathan arrived home and gave the good news to his father. He also lit a joss stick and quietly placed it in the surgery. It was a refreshing smell after the sweat and stink of too many bodies, toing and froing throughout the day and of course the king had to be kept clean.

Doctor Jonathan kept an eye on the king whilst Lt Fitzwilliam went out to the toilets. He checked his breathing and felt his pulse. Then he felt the king's foot. It was warm and Jonathan thought he felt a slight twitch as he made the examination. He felt again but there was nothing. He then lifted an eyelid to see if there was any response. Suddenly as he looked down at the king, both eyelids flicked open.

Jonathan was taken aback. "Your Majesty, are you awake, can you hear me?" The eyelids fluttered open and shut a couple of times before remaining open. "Where am I?" muttered the king.

Jonathan looked to see if Lieutenant Fitzwilliam was anywhere to be seen. "Your Majesty has had a bad riding accident, please sire do not move you have severe injuries."

"Who are you?" muttered the king.

"Sire, I am Doctor Jonathan Godwin and you are in my surgery." The king's eyes fluttered and then closed. Jonathan was a bit panicky and anxious for Lt Fitzwilliam to return. The military doctor appeared and could see that Jonathan was a bit flustered. "What's happened?" he asked. Jonathan could hardly get the words out. "He just woke up and spoke to me."

Lt Fitzwilliam quickly began to examine the king. "Well, he's not awake now, he's still unconscious, what did he say?"

Jonathan looked at Lt Fitzwilliam. "He just asked *where am I and who are you* and then closed his eyes again. I wish you had been here to see." The military doctor told Jonathan that sometimes temporary consciousness does occur and it was a good sign. The king's own doctors will be told of this and may decide to try and bring the king around but he preferred to let nature take its course. If they bring him around too soon, he will be trying to move around and may cause more injury.

Lord Hastings asked Jonathan what the king had said and for how long the king had been conscious. The four doctors stepped to one side and held a discussion. Nothing was said to Jonathan or Lt Fitzwilliam. They allowed the orderlies to change the king and to wash him before they gathered around the bed and started to address him. After half an hour, there had been no response so they left him alone. Mrs Godwin was allowed to feed him liquid refreshments. Later that afternoon, the king's doctors decided they wanted to move him to Boughey Hall and more comfortable surroundings. They asked Doctor Godwin if he had a suitable board that they could place under his majesty to support him rigidly ready for transportation. The backboard already in place was not quite suitable; something longer would be needed to support the whole body. Doctor John asked how they were going to transport him to Boughey Hall which was four miles away. The king's doctors said Lord Fairbanks had an open carriage he could use and a stout board placed across the seats would suffice. Doctor John said it would be a bumpy ride as the roads were a bit uneven in places. He suggested lots of cushions be placed on the seats to soften the ride.

Lord Fairbanks arrived with his coach which had been adapted to take the king to Boughey Hall. Mrs Godwin wrapped the king in blankets to keep him warm and watched as four soldiers lifted him up and carried him outside. The board was placed across the seats with the cushions in place. Two of the doctors found enough room to sit in the coach with the king. Slowly, the horses were led onto the road carrying their precious passenger. The king's guard escorted the coach and Lord Fairbanks and the remaining doctors followed in another coach. Doctor John and Jonathan watched as they departed. A sigh of relief escaped their lips as the responsibility left them. Mrs Godwin began cleaning the surgery.

Lady Patricia looked on as the coach party came slowly up the drive to the front door. The butler and staff were outside awaiting the party, unsure as to what orders they were to be given.

Sir James Godfrey had returned with his men to the ranges and gave orders for half the camp to be dismantled and the supply wagons loaded. The company was split into two sections. One section was to accompany the wagons to Boughey Hall whilst the other section remained under the command of Captain Marshall and continue practising with the new muskets. The section accompanying the wagons would establish a camp in the grounds of Boughey Hall to protect the king under the command of Sir James Godfrey. Lt Fitzwilliam would remain at the ranges.

The stretcher-bearers gently lifted the king out of the carriage under the supervision of Lords Percival and Hastings. Captains Howard and Perrie were taken upstairs to where his majesty would be staying. It was a large room with views over the river. Captain Howard examined the large bed which had been adjusted by placing a very large board under the mattress. Every instruction had been carried out for the king's stay. The stretcher was carried into the room and placed on the bed. Following instructions from the doctors, the king was gently eased off the stretcher onto the board. They then started examining the unconscious monarch and did all that they could to assure his comfort.

Doctor John and Doctor Jonathan were very pleased with themselves and Mrs Godwin poured them all a glass of wine. "We did very well under the circumstances but Jonathan, my dear, no more patients for a while."

Doctor John said he would be off to an early start in the morning another meeting with the noble gentlemen at Western Towers had been arranged and Doctor John and the architect would be discussing the plans and the cost. "It's a pity it wasn't ready for the king's visit; he could have been our first patient and then maybe a royal grant would have been made." They all laughed at Doctor John's comment.

Jonathan would do the morning surgery and Mrs Godwin would do the afternoon one allowing Jonathan to visit the convent again and any other calls he had on his round. After a hot drink, they all retired for the night. It had been an exciting day but they were all glad it was over.

Jonathan ate his breakfast and waved goodbye to his father who had risen early and was about to leave for Western Towers.

Jonathan instructed Edward that he would need his horse after lunch. Meanwhile, he tended to the surgery. It wasn't a busy morning, only the odd person popping in to have injuries redressed. Usually, it was the farm labourers or their families but there were the occasional travellers passing through Rugeley that made up sufficient funds to pay for the running costs. The private patients, business people, and the town's shopping community, all helped maintain a healthy income.

Doctor John greeted the noble gentry at Western Towers. Everyone was there even Lord Fairbanks who Doctor John had least expected to see. He made a beeline for the doctor confirming that all was well at Boughey Hall but no, there hadn't been any further developments. Lord Fairbanks told Doctor John that he had confided with his fellow men regarding the cost of developing Western Towers and most of them were at least willing to listen. The architect displayed the plans for all to see on the table in the library where everyone could see them. Doctor John encouraged all the gentry to examine the plans and ask questions which would be answered where possible.

After the examination of the plans, Doctor John asked the noblemen to be seated. He had already made it known that he was looking for more money from them and handed out slips of paper for them to write on. "If you can increase your original donation, it will be a great help to this project. The original sum donated has been swallowed up by the extensive work needed to be carried out and leaves little to pay for the staff required to run this project. It is hoped that at some time it will be able to finance itself and this will certainly be looked into as we proceed but first, let's dig a little deeper into our pockets and get things moving."

The noblemen started deliberating amongst themselves, not all were keen on parting with any more money. Doctor John organised drinks and light refreshments. After half an hour, the meeting was called to order and Doctor John asked for the slips of paper to be collected. He scanned them quickly. Thanking them for their generosity, he said that work would start immediately. He also stated that all would receive updates on how the work was proceeding and also notification of all monies donated.

There had been no mention of the special visitor at Boughey Hall and Doctor John was pleased that Lord Fairbanks had not mentioned it.

Mrs Godwin prepared lunch after the surgery had closed and was pleased to see her husband dismounting his horse. He had a pleased look on his face as he sat down at the table. Jonathan noticed and asked his father how the meeting had gone. Doctor John smiled and said, "We are ready to start work on the project. The nobles parted with a little more cash and now Doctor John had ordered the architect to find suitable builders and carpenters to start immediately."

Mrs Godwin sat down at the table and joined in the conversation. "It's a pity that only the landed gentry can afford such an undertaking, the poor people around this area could benefit from a similar luxury." Doctor John agreed with his caring wife. "But they don't have the money, my dear, that's the difference, money can buy you things."

Jonathan made his excuses and looked out the window just as Edward led his horse up to the house. He could still smell the lavender coming from the surgery as he closed the door behind him. There was a slight drizzle in the air as he made his way up the hill to the convent. Sister Mary opened the door and led Jonathan to the isolation word where she handed him over to the nuns caring for the patients. Jonathan was given a mask to protect him. He made straight for the soldier who was sitting on his bed. "You look a lot better than when we brought you in," said the doctor looking at the patient.

"Oh yes, Doctor, I'm a lot better, thanks to you and the nuns." The soldier allowed Jonathan to carry out a thorough medical examination. His breathing was almost normal, his eyes were no longer discharging, and the colour in his cheeks almost normal. He gave an occasional cough but nothing really pronounced. "Yes, you are getting better," said Jonathan, "are you still applying the cream to your chest and back?" The soldier reached for the jar. "Almost gone, Doctor." The fragrance in the air still lingered as Doctor Jonathan visited each patient. The others weren't as bright as the soldier so he decided to treat the gipsy girl and Squire

Brindley's daughter the same way as he treated the soldier but he had to visit Brother Thomas for more supplies.

Thanking the nuns for their help, he made his way down the hill onto the main road. It was still drizzling but his coat was keeping him dry, he simply pulled up his collar and pulled down his hat.

Brother Thomas was just returning from prayers in the monastery when Jonathan walked through the garden of herbs and plants to the monk's workshop. He was greeted courteously and of course, offered a warm drink to keep the cold away. Jonathan licked his lips. "What is this one, Thomas?" The monk smiled and said, "Rosehip syrup and honey to keep the cold away." Jonathan asked his friend for some more of the paste, explaining that it was helping to fight the chest infection and that he was extending his trials to two more patients. Brother Thomas also offered a bunch of joss sticks of various fragrances for Jonathan to try out. "Only country and herbal fragrances doctor, no harm in them." Jonathan walked around the workshop and stopped to look at the skeleton. "My friend interests you, Doctor," said Brother Thomas. Jonathan thought about the king and his injuries. "What do the Chinese recommend for back and neck injuries?" Brother Thomas reached the skeleton down and lay it on the table. "First, as you know yourself, you must define the injury. Is it merely a bruised body or had there been any real damage done. Of course with an injury, there will be severe swelling which makes it difficult to see or feel anything. So you must wait until the swelling diminishes. Then you can begin your investigations by looking and feeling for any deformity. If there are broken bones, you will see them and feel them. If it is internal then you must look at the patient and see how he holds himself. Now I will show you how to feel. Close your eyes and feel down the spine." Jonathan did as Brother Thomas instructed him, feeling from the neck down. "What did you feel?" Jonathan said he just felt a normal bone structure. "That's because there's nothing wrong with this spine," said Brother Thomas. "Now keep your eyes closed and try again." He made an adjustment to the skeleton. Doctor Jonathan again examined the spine pausing to feeling a couple of places more carefully. "Now what do you feel, Doctor?" Jonathan ran his fingers over the spine again. "There are at least two discs out of line, I think." Brother Thomas guided Jonathan's fingers over the spine. "At least three, Jonathan which would cause a lot of pain and discomfort making it impossible for a person to stand up or move at all. Now feel the neck itself, close your eyes again." Jonathan felt around the neck area feeling the construction of the bones. This time he wasn't sure. Brother Thomas told him to stop and made an adjustment. "Now try again." This time Jonathan did notice something was different but wasn't sure what it was. "Look Jonathan," said Brother Thomas, "nothing broken but a nerve trapped can cause a lot of pain and can obstruct the movement of the head." Jonathan had done some basic examinations on skeletons during his medical training but what Brother Thomas was teaching him was more intense and informative. "The Chinese were very good at manipulation and massage and used needles to ease certain problems but my training was interrupted and I had to leave so I never learnt about the needles but I will return one day and continue my learning."

Jonathan thanked him for showing him the skeleton and said he had found it very interesting. "But the swelling and the bruising must be treated first." Brother Thomas agreed. "After the swelling has gone, you can begin to investigate the body but be very gentle because you can't see inside the patient, as you know there are nerves going through the spine all the way down the body."

Jonathan told Brother Thomas that he had a patient who had had a riding accident and couldn't move. He didn't reveal who the patient was and Brother Thomas didn't ask. "Such accidents can prove fatal especially if the neck is broken and if the spine is damaged the patient may never walk again. Treatment is very delicate and can take a long time. Getting the patient to cooperate is also very difficult and frustrating." Brother Thomas gave Jonathan a jar of cream. "This may help ease the swelling." Jonathan asked for some of the other creams that Thomas had given him, telling the monk how good it had been.

Jonathan revisited the convent and handed over the cream to one of the nuns looking after the sick with instructions to only treat the two patients he had specified and then he made his way home to a hearty meal. He hadn't planned on going out that evening but a sudden urge to see Lady Patricia came over him. He made his excuses and went to his room to change. Mrs Godwin looked at Doctor John and smiled, she knew where Jonathan was going although he hadn't said.

The butler opened the door to Jonathan's knock, greeting him cordially. "Lady Patricia is in the drawing room, Doctor, she has had a busy day today looking after our visitors." Lady Patricia looked up as Jonathan entered the room. A smile crossed her lips. "Oh, Jonathan, what a lovely surprise! I wasn't expecting you." Jonathan took her outstretched hand and kissed it. "I just felt like some pleasant company, Patricia,

I hope you don't mind my sudden intrusion." She beckoned him to sit by her and moved closer to him. He asked how her day had been and if there was any news about the king. She said she only went up at meal times to feed him. His doctors were keeping a close watch on him but they seemed to be getting impatient. She had overheard them mention getting the king back to London as soon as possible. "They mustn't move him yet it's too early," said Jonathan, "his injuries are less than a week old, they haven't had time to heal yet. They could kill him if they move him too quickly and he would never survive the journey to London." Lady Patricia nodded her head understanding what Jonathan had just said. "I will be going up again shortly, would you like to accompany me?"

Jonathan carried the tray of food whilst Lady Patricia carried the bowl of warm water and towels. "I always give him a wash before his supper. I think it may help if he knows we are there." Lord Percival and Lord Hastings were on duty when they entered the bedroom. They greeted Doctor Jonathan briefly and stepped aside to let Lady Patricia approach the king's bedside. "Is there any improvement?" Jonathan asked. Both doctors shook their heads. Jonathan looked at the king as he lay unconscious. The two doctors excused themselves as they needed the toilets. Lady Patricia finished her task and moved away allowing Jonathan a closer look at the king. His breathing was still a bit erratic, Jonathan felt his pulse, still a bit fast. His hands were warm. Jonathan looked at his bare feet and felt them. There was no movement until Jonathan ran his finger down the sole of the left foot. There was a slight twitch. Jonathan lifted the eyelids and noticed a slight flickering. "Can you hear me, your majesty?" he asked. He held the king's hand. "Squeeze my hand if you can hear me, sire." He gently rubbed the king's hand and noticed a faint effort to squeeze his hand. "It is me, Doctor Jonathan sire, do you remember me?" The eyes fluttered and opened briefly. "Doctor Jonathan, yes." His eyes closed again. Lady Patricia said, "He's responding to you Jonathan." The king's doctors returned and took up their positions on either side of the king's bed. Jonathan asked if they were doing anything to rouse the king. They said apart from talking to him and checking his breathing they would wait a little longer before they decided whether to get the king back to London. "It's too early for that," said Jonathan, "to try and move him so soon could kill him. Let him stay here until he comes around. It could take weeks but I strongly advise you not to move him, besides the journey alone could kill him, let nature take its course, he will be well looked after here." The doctors looked at Jonathan, surprised by his outburst. "We are the king's doctors sir, it will be our decision not yours." Jonathan was angry. "And it will be your responsibility if the king dies." He gave them an angry look and left the room.

"Impertinent young scoundrel," exclaimed Lord Percival, "who does he think he is!" Lord Hastings coughed and spluttered, "Just a young upstart with very little experience, we will decide not him."

Lady Patricia followed Jonathan downstairs. "Take no notice of them, Jonathan, they don't know everything. I'll have a word with uncle; he may be able to influence them."

Doctor Jonathan bade farewell to Patricia, his temper subsided. "I wish the king could stay awake a little longer so I may talk to him." Lady Patricia planted a kiss on his cheek.

Lord Hagleigh was in a foul mood. Samuel hadn't been doing anything towards running the business for weeks since his encounter with the burglars and the loss of his sword hand. He had become more moody and depressed. His father had tried talking to him but he just wasn't listening. "Why don't you take a holiday or something? Visit some of your old friends in London. Find yourself a nice elegant Lady or something. Forget Lady Patricia, she's not for you. Samuel, you have got to pull yourself together, we need you in the business; it's too much for Brother Matthew to run on his own." Samuel reached for his wine glass and refilled it. His father's ranting was driving him mad. Why can't everybody just leave him alone to drown his sorrows? "Maybe I will go to London, it's terribly boring around here," he said finally.

The surgery bell rang and Mrs Godwin went to let in the first patient of the day. Doctor John was looking at the plans for the alterations being carried out at Western Towers. Doctor Jonathan was looking through his medical notes from his days at medical school, looking for treatments for back injuries. He was convinced that if they decided to move the king too soon would cause him more harm and probably be fatal.

Lord Fairbanks and his clerk were looking through the paperwork which detailed the accounts of all the landowners and businesses who paid taxes to the crown. Whether or not, his majesty would ever be in a fit state to see them was yet to be seen but still they had to be prepared.

Lady Patricia carried the washbasin and tray upstairs to the king's room. The king's physicians were in attendance, not doing anything in particular just looking and talking. They stepped aside to let Lady Patricia carry out the task of washing the king's face and hands. A full body wash was carried out by the medical orderlies every other day or when it was necessary to clean him. Captain Howard suggested they leave Lady Patricia to carry out her duties whilst he and Captain Perrie went downstairs for a quick breakfast. They gave instructions to be called immediately if anything should happen. A servant girl brought in a tray with liquid food for the king. She placed the tray on a table and waited for Lady Patricia to finish washing the king. She then took away the bowl of water and towels. Lady Patricia sat at the side of the bed. "Your majesty, I am now going to feed you," she said quietly and began putting the spoon to his mouth. She gasped in amazement as the king's eyes fluttered. "Your majesty can you hear me, if you can, open your eyes for me."

She watched as again the eyes fluttered and then opened. "Where am I?" he asked.

Patricia said, "You are at Boughey Hall, sire but you have had a bad accident. Shall I fetch your doctors?"

The king tried to give a weak smile. "No, I'm sick of listening to them, who are you?"

Lady Patricia held his hand. "I'm Lord Fairbank's niece, Lady Patricia, I'm just giving you some liquid food, shall we carry on before it goes cold?"

The king looked at Lady Patricia. "I remember you from long ago when I last visited your father and uncle. You lost your mother and father, didn't you?"

Lady Patricia nodded her head. "Yes, sire, they were lost in South America somewhere."

The king took the food willingly. "You have grown into a beautiful woman, Patricia, those doctors of mine want to get me back to London as soon as possible but that young doctor Jonathan says it is too soon to move me. I don't know what to do, I can't move at all. I've heard them say I may be paralysed for life."

Lady Patricia squeezed his hand. "Don't let them move you yet, sire, Doctor Jonathan is a good doctor. It has only been a week since your accident; it's too soon for you to travel. Let Doctor Jonathan decide for you."

The king closed his eyes again temporarily. "Don't tell my doctors I've come around, Patricia. I'll pretend I'm still unconscious, only you and Doctor Jonathan will be able to talk to me." The door opened and the king's doctors entered the room. Patricia picked up the tray and left the room.

Lady Isabella greeted Doctor John; she had taken over the east wing and was still settling herself into her new surroundings. The alterations had been carried out and now she was getting used to the different doors and her exit from her lounge to the walk along the river. "It will take a while, Doctor John but I'm sure I will adapt. It's a better view of the river from here and easily accessible. My staff have accepted their new accommodation so all is well."

Doctor John took her hand and led her through the French windows into the garden. "I'm sure this will be better for you, my lady, it is nice and compact and this is a nice walk along the river. There will be a small garden with roses and such for you to look at through your window and to sit in during the summer months." Lady Isabella thanked the doctor for his care and consideration. "And when I am gone, you can also have the east wing, Doctor."

Chapter 5

Jonathan and his father decided to visit the schools again just to see if there had been any more children with chest infections. They were pleased to see there wasn't and so they continued their journey up to the convent. The mother superior greeted the doctors and enquired whether any new cases had been reported. She told the doctors that the convent nuns were handling the situation very well and the patients seemed to be stabilised. She escorted them through the corridors to the isolation ward. As they walked around checking on the patients, Jonathan noticed that the soldier was out of bed and looking quite well. He explained to his father that he had been using the soldier as a guinea pig trying out the medicines Brother Thomas had given him. He examined the soldier who said he was feeling very well indeed.

Jonathan visited the other two patients who he had treated. The gipsy girl was still looking poorly but her coughing had subdued according to the nuns but she seemed a bit brighter.

Lady Brindley's daughter was looking a bit better but still coughing. Jonathan told the nuns to carry on with the treatment and to put joss sticks around the ward to freshen up the air. He would call in again next week and if there was an improvement, he would begin the treatment on the remaining patients. Doctor John asked Jonathan why he thought the soldier had responded more than the others. Jonathan said he had been treating the soldier longer and he hoped the rest of the patients would respond when they were all given the same treatment. He told his father that he was learning a lot from Brother Thomas. "Of course, he is very knowledgeable, he's been to lots of places and has been taught very well but his medical skills are different to ours and maybe we can learn from him," said Doctor John.

Lord Hagleigh watched as his son Samuel packed his bags. "It's good as you are getting away for a while, I'm sure the break will do you good and London is bustling at this time of year but let us know you are safe." A quick handshake and Samuel got into his father's coach. The driver had already been given instructions.

Lord Hagleigh spoke to his younger son Matthew, "It will be a bit harder for you in his absence but I'll make sure someone helps you out. I don't know when we will see Samuel again." Lady Hagleigh dried her eyes. "He hasn't been the same since that Lady Patricia turned him down, I shall not forgive her for this."

Lady Patricia did not mention her talk with the king, she merely wrote a note to Jonathan asking him to visit her as soon as possible. She asked the butler to see that one of the servants delivered the note at once.

Mrs Godwin looked up as the horseman approached the surgery. She didn't recognise him but took the letter offered by him addressed to Doctor Jonathan Godwin and marked 'urgent'. It was almost lunchtime but neither of the doctors had yet returned. She put the letter on the table in Jonathan's place. It wasn't long before the two doctors were handing over their horses to Edward who led them to the stables. Mrs

Godwin greeted her husband and son and then pointed out to Jonathan that he had received a letter delivered by hand. He opened the letter and read the contents, "I must give lunch a miss, Mother, Lady Patricia wants to see me urgently, I must dash off." Doctor John looked a bit perplexed. "I hope nothing has happened to the king."

Jonathan rode his horse over the fields taking the shortcut to Boughey Hall. The guards on duty let him through instantly recognising him. The butler showed Jonathan into the library and said he would notify Lady Patricia of his arrival. He had hardly sat down when Patricia entered the library. Her face was bursting with excitement when she told Jonathan of her conversation with the king. "He knew who I was," she blurted out, "he remembered me from his last visit all these years ago and he mentioned you, Jonathan, come with me when I take his food to him any moment now. Talk to him but he will only talk when his doctors are not present."

The tray was laden and Jonathan escorted Patricia to the king's room. His doctors greeted him but made no effort to converse with him. Patricia told the doctors she would like to feed the king before his meal cooled down and if they wanted to take advantage of a break they could do so. They said they would but looked at Jonathan. "The king is fine, do not interfere." Jonathan acknowledged their warning.

When they had left the room, Lady Patricia sat beside the bed ready to feed the king. "Your Majesty, it is Lady Patricia, I've come to feed you, are you awake?" She touched his hand and stroked it. "Sire, Doctor Jonathan has come to see you, are you awake?"

She watched as the king's eyes began to flutter. "I am but you sound far away."

Lady Patricia stroked his brow. "It's all these medicines they are giving you for the pain, they will make you sleepy, I've brought Doctor Jonathan to see you."

Jonathan sat on the edge of the bed. "Your Majesty, you have had a bad riding accident and have received back and neck injuries. They are giving you pain relief medication that will make you sleepy."

The king opened his eyes. "They are talking about moving me to London, Doctor but I am still in a lot of pain, I can't move my legs or my head."

Jonathan spoke to Patricia, "They must not move him yet, it's far too early, his injuries are unknown as yet because we can't move him to conduct any examinations, he must remain as he is until all the swelling has gone, at least another two weeks."

"Your Majesty they will not listen to me. You must tell them to let you rest a while longer before they try to move you. Sire, they will only listen to you."

The king closed his eyes and then opened them again. "I will try, Doctor but if they see I'm regaining consciousness, they will be trying all sorts of things."

Jonathan said that if Lady Patricia was present, she would be able to see what they do. Jonathan addressed the king, "Sire, you must tell them it is too soon to move you, they will not listen to me. Tell them you are still in a lot of pain and you cannot be moved yet. Ask them to treat your bed sores for a start. Your broken leg hasn't healed yet and you are still very fragile. You need a lot more rest before they try to move you." The king said he would try but he said he would wait a little longer before he opened his eyes for them.

Sir James Godfrey looked at his soldiers as they returned from the ranges. He called to Captain Marshall. "I think that tomorrow we will march to Boughey Hall and change the guard there, Captain. Give these men some rest and bring the other troops back for more firing practice. I also want to see if the doctors will allow them to visit the town yet, they need some recreation."

Richard Turpin reined Bess into the courtyard of the Wayfarers Inn on the great north road and handed his horse over to the stable hand with instructions to have his horse fed and watered and given a comfortable stall. He then walked into the inn and asked for a room. The innkeeper looked at him and asked how long he would be staying. Turpin said that as a courier he could only stay one night as his job entailed dispatches urgently delivered. The innkeeper seemed satisfied and asked if anything else was required. Turpin eyed the barmaid and gave her a smile, then asked if food could be sent up to his room. He nodded and winked at the innkeeper. "Any form of comfort would be appreciated," he said.

Doctor Jonathan sat in the drawing room at Boughey Hall waiting for Lady Patricia to join him. She had to oversee the feeding of her guests as Lord Fairbanks entertained them. She waited for them to be seated and the food was being served before making her excuses to leave the table on some pretence. She joined Jonathan in the library and told him that she had heard Lord Percival and Lord Hastings making plans to return to London but she didn't know all the details but would find out from her uncle later. Jonathan said he wished they would all go and leave the king in his care. "They will cripple him if they are not careful, he's in a very delicate condition," he said. Lady Patricia held onto his arm as

Jonathan decided to leave. "I'll see you soon, my lady." She tugged at his arm. "I am Patricia to you, Jonathan Godwin." He gave a huge smile. "And always will be." He kissed her lightly on the cheek before climbing into the saddle and heading for home.

Mrs Godwin asked if he had eaten. He shook his head as he sat down at the table. "No, Mother, I've been too busy to think of food." Doctor John entered the room. "How are things, Jonathan?" He looked at his parents and said in a pleasant tone. "I've just been talking to the king." Doctor John placed his hands on Jonathan's shoulders. "That's good news, Jonathan and how is his majesty?" Mrs Godwin placed the food on the table and listened to what Jonathan was saying. "The king comes in and out of consciousness to suit himself. He speaks to me and Lady Patricia only. His doctors have told me not to interfere so we can only converse with the king when they let Lady Patricia feed him and they leave the room and take a break. He says he hears them talking between themselves and believes they are planning to take him to London. I've already told them it is too early for such an undertaking but again I've been told not to interfere." Doctor John agreed it was too early to move him and the journey to London could cause devastating injury to the king. "I shall try my best to convince them to let the king rest a little longer," said Jonathan, "but they are the king's physicians and they outrank me."

Richard Turpin woke to the sound of a cockerel crowing. It was barely light. He turned over and felt for his comforter but she had already flown the coup. The tray had gone but she had left the rose lying on the table. Richard smiled, what did he expect 'seconds'. He rose and washed and dressed. There was a light knock on the door, opening if he found a tray on the floor with cereal and toasted bread.

The innkeeper was just disappearing down the stairs. Richard ate the food and put on his cloak. It was now daylight and he wanted to make an early start, he nodded to the innkeeper as he left the inn. The stable hand had saddled Bess and was leading her out into the courtyard. A sovereign tip and Richard was on his way to London. It was still a good ride but the weather was fair.

Doctor John and Doctor Jonathan were already on to the road to Western Towers. Doctor John was anxious to see how the work was going on. He had promised Lady Isabella that he would oversee the alterations and make sure she wasn't disturbed in any way. After that, he was going to visit Lord Hagleigh. Jonathan was to visit two patients on the outskirts of Rugeley and he would also call on the gipsy family if they were still camped outside the town and from there he wanted to visit Brother Thomas at the monastery. He hoped that by lunchtime he would have completed his rounds with a quick visit to the convent, and from there to Boughey Hall. He wanted to try and befriend the king's doctors and not to antagonise them.

He dismounted and after checking in with the king's guards, he wrapped on the large oak door at Boughey Hall. The butler answered and showed him into the library. Lady Patricia appeared within minutes. "I didn't think I would see you today, Jonathan, I know your time is precious but it's good to see you."

Jonathan took her outstretched hand. "It's always good to see you, my lady," he said with a cheeky smile, "are you ready to feed his majesty?" She said the food was being prepared right away. "Come Jonathan, help me carry the tray." They climbed the staircase and knocked lightly on the king's bedroom door. Captain Howard opened the door and greeted Lady Patricia courteously. He gave Jonathan a nod and let them into the room. "How is his majesty today?" asked Jonathan, making it into a friendly question by smiling at the king's doctor. Captain Howard looked at Jonathan. "Still no change." Jonathan said he once had a patient who had a similar fall and had been unconscious for three weeks before finally waking up. The surgeon looked at Jonathan surprised. "So you have had an experience of this sort of thing?" he asked. Jonathan said he had and in the country accidents like this were common amongst the farming community. "There was always some farmer falling off a haystack or falling from the top floor of his barn, and then the horse riding fraternity amongst the nobles who drink too much wine and still think they can hunt foxes. Oh yes, we see this sort of thing regularly." Jonathan spoke casually to the doctor hoping he sounded convincing. In fact, he had only treated one such casualty and it was due to excess drink that the patient received little damage only to his pride. The doctors left the room to lunch with Lord Fairbanks, Percival and Hastings. Patricia was sitting close to the king feeding him the warm broth and talking softly to him. Jonathan took his pulse, it was practically normal and his breathing was stable. He went to the foot of the bed and took hold of the king's foot. He ran his finger up and down the sole noticing some slight twitching. The king opened his eyes. "Ah! My two friends, I am pleased to see you. I am getting bored lying here like this and my body aches like mad. How long am I going to be like this, Doctor Jonathan? I have heard them talking and they are saying I may be paralysed for life. Please tell me, Doctor Jonathan that this will not be so." Jonathan sat by the side of the king. "I do not think you will be paralysed, sire, you have reflexes in your foot which are good signs but it is going to be quite a while and will take a lot of massaging and stimulation to get things moving again. Your broken leg will take weeks to mend. Only with expert nursing will we ever know how you will recover. I want to help but your surgeons have warned me not to interfere." The door opened and Doctor Hastings and Howard entered. "The king closed his eyes and resumed unconsciousness. Lady Patricia informed them that the king was taking his food well. Captain Howard addressed Jonathan and Lady Patricia. "Lord Percival and Lord Hastings have decided to go back to London and have a special coach built to transport the king back to London. That will take a couple of weeks so we will be staying here for a least that time, who knows the king may come around by then. In the meantime, we will monitor his progress and administer pain killers. His bedsores are being looked at."

Jonathan commented that the king was in good hands and if there was anything he could do to help he would make himself available.

Lady Patricia was very pleased, she said that Jonathan had conducted himself well. "Uncle may be going on his rounds in a few days time. He has to visit all the gentry in the area for assessment and to collect taxes for the king. I want some soldiers to go with him as he has to collect a substantial sum of money." Jonathan said the officer in charge would allocate soldiers to escort Lord Fairbanks and he would have a word with him before he left. Lady Patricia squeezed his hand.

"Thank you, Jonathan, please come again soon, I'm happy when you are here with me."

Jonathan reined his horse to where the soldiers were camped. He was directed to the guard commander Lieutenant Middleton. Jonathan informed him of Lord Fairbanks duties and asked if a guard could be provided as this was the king's business that Lord Fairbanks was undertaking. The Lieutenant said he would confer with Sir James Godfrey who was already on his way to Boughey hall to change the guard and he said that something would be arranged.

Dick Turpin made his way through the streets of London. He was making his way to an inn down the back streets frequented by his old comrades. He tethered Bess to the rail and entered the inn. A joyous shout of "look who's here" greeted him by half a dozen shady looking characters known as 'The Essex Gang'. John King stood up and greeted his old partner with a hug and a handshake. "Dick me, old mate, you've come back to us, I bet you missed the excitement and the boys eh!" Dick said his journey up north had been a waste of time and he was yearning to get back on the road again. John King said that he and the boys had one or two things lined up and Dick was welcome to join in with them.

Lord Samuel Hagleigh spent his time in London at his cousin's apartment in Mayfair. His cousin was the son of Lord Hagleigh's brother who was in the banking business. Sir Robert Hagleigh was wealthy and had properties all over London. He spoilt his offsprings and all three of his children had their own place in the city. John Hagleigh was abroad at the moment so his apartment was empty and available to his cousin Lord Samuel so were a number of socialites who enjoyed a decadent way of life. Samuel soon made their acquaintances and began to enjoy a way of life he hadn't endured for many years. He mixed with the gentry, many of which were high ranking army officers. He was soon 'one of the boys' enjoying the high society life. He soon made friends with Captain Blaine an artillery officer in the service of the king. He would entertain Lord Samuel with his tales of exciting battles and tours abroad. Samuel listened, and it sounded very exciting and soon began asking how he could become part of it. Captain Blaine fuelled his enthusiasm by inviting Samuel to the military barracks just south of the city and could arrange a meeting with his commanding officer if Samuel was interested, there were always vacancies for artillery officers. It sounded far more exciting than running his father's mineral businesses and Samuel was eager to join.

Jonathan was up early he was looking after the surgery this morning while Doctor John visited Western Towers and two local patients. He would then take over from Doctor Jonathan who was making a visit to the convent and patients out of town and then call into Boughey Hall.

Mrs Godwin would take the float into town and do the shopping, calling in on farms for the milk and eggs which were always fresher than on the market.

Sir James Godfrey led his company of soldiers through the forest and over the fields to Boughey Hall to change the guards. He was wondering how many more times he would be doing this before he could get back to training the full company. He had other companies in London waiting to be trained with the new muskets. The French army could be on their doorstep before the battalion of marksmen were ready for them. The king wanted a thousand marksmen ready and waiting to fight off the French if they decided to invade, but now the king had upset the whole training programme by getting rolled on by his horse.

The commander of the half company of soldiers protecting his majesty waited for Sir John to arrive, he had been asked to supply a guard for Lord Fairbanks on his rounds which would take at least a week for him to complete.

Doctor John made his tour of Western Towers. He could see the vast alterations were well underway and the architect was adamant that they were ahead of schedule.

Lady Isabella sent word for the doctor to call on her when he had finished and arranged for a light snack to be there when he came in. Doctor John entered the drawing room with a broad smile on his face. "Always a pleasure to see you, my lady," he said reaching out for her hand and kissing it. Lady Isabella asked her maid to pour the drinks. "I'm not ill, Doctor I just wanted to have a little chat that's all. I don't see many people these days. Friends seem to avoid visiting when you get old." Doctor John said he always enjoyed a little chat when he came to Western Towers and told Lady Isabella that she was looking well. He said that he had noticed that people do notice the loneliness as they mature, especially when they lose their husband or wife. "Of course, you could always find a companion to come and stay with you," he said, "you still have plenty of room on the East wing."

Doctor John had collected the money from the nobles and opened a bank account through a solicitor and arranged documents to be given to each nobleman as a receipt and indicating that the said recipient had bought into the Western Towers infirmary and was entitled to medical treatment for him and his family free of charge. He was pleased with the way things were going. Now he had to set up a reception, a consulting room and a dispensary plus a section for staff to be housed. There were some resident nurses but most were living around the area close to Western Towers. Mrs Godwin, being an experienced and most qualified nurse was appointed head of the nursing staff and was responsible for training. She enjoyed the responsibility and fitted in between Doctor John and Doctor Jonathan, taking turns to look after the surgery back home.

The nuns at the convent noticed an improvement in those receiving the special treatment and the soldier was already fit enough to be discharged but not until the doctor said so.

It had been almost a week since Lord Percival and Lord Hastings had departed for London. Lady Patricia and Doctor Jonathan had kept up their lunchtime appointment with the king and had several secret talks with him. Jonathan had seen a slight improvement in his majesty, he was more coherent during their talks, he was now wondering if it was time to wake him up so that the doctors could try to examine him further; it had now been three weeks since the king's accident.

Lady Patricia was waiting for Jonathan when he arrived at Boughey Hall. The guard commander approached him as he rode up the driveway. Lieutenant Middleton informed him that a four-man guard had been made available to escort Lord Fairbanks on his journey. Doctor Jonathan thanked him and said he would inform his lordship. Lady Patricia gave Doctor Jonathan a warm welcome and she collected the king's lunch and made their way upstairs. The two doctors greeted them and left them to feed the king. Jonathan watched as the patient took his food with an occasional flicker of his eyelids. Jonathan sat on the side of the bed. "Sire, are you awake. It is Doctor Jonathan and Lady Patricia." The king slowly opened his eyes. "I'm still very drowsy," he said, "yes Sire, it is the medication, perhaps it is time now to ease it off except for the painkillers. You do seem to have made some improvement. I would suggest, Sire that now it is time for you to wake up and confer with your doctors. They need to examine you more thoroughly now." The king looked at Jonathan. "If you think, I will be alright with them but I want you to stay as well." Jonathan said he would but didn't think the king's own doctors would allow it. "I will speak to them, Doctor Jonathan." Lady Patricia was taking the tray away. "Will you tell the doctors to come up right away?" asked Jonathan.

Captain Howard and Captain Perrie entered the room. "What is it, Doctor?" they asked. Jonathan replied, "The king is waking up, I've spoken to him." They both stood at the bedside as Jonathan addressed the king. "Sire, your doctors are here, can you open your eyes for them?" His eyes fluttered and gradually opened. "Doctor Jonathan, will you stay?" he asked. The two doctors looked at the king. "Your majesty, it's Captain Howard and Perrie, we are here with you now. You have regained consciousness, at last, now we can examine you more thoroughly and ascertain your injuries." The king looked at them. "Let Doctor Jonathan assist you, he seems to know what he's doing." The two doctors looked at Jonathan and nodded approval. Jonathan suggested the examinations would be carried out later when the orderlies had carried out their duties of washing the king and changing any soiled clothing. The doctors agreed and conferred with the king. "What do you propose we do first, Doctor Jonathan?" Captain Perrie asked. "I suggest we remove the neck support and see if his majesty can move his head. If he can do that, we raise him slightly and examine him for any neck trauma. If he is alright then we move further down the spine. Let's take it from there." Jonathan waited for their approval, saying the examination should be slow and easy.

Lord Hagleigh read the letter delivered that morning and started shouting angrily. Lady Hagleigh came running into the drawing room to see what was the matter. "The young fool has joined the military," he said waving the letter. "Of all the foolish things he could do, he's gone and enlisted in the army." Lady Hagleigh wiped away the tears. "It's all that Lady Patricia's fault for turning him down. I'll never forgive her for this. If my beloved Samuel gets killed, I'll have her head." Lord Hagleigh shook his head in disbelief. "It's my fault, I told him to go to London and enjoy himself but I never thought he would do this."

Lord Fairbanks and his clerk got into the carriage. Two guards got in with them and another sat beside the driver. "Well, at least we should be safe," said the clerk. Lord Fairbanks waved to his niece as the coach pulled away. "About a week," he shouted to her. She went back into the house and waited for Jonathan to join her in the drawing room. "You will be staying here overnight?" she asked. He said he would have to go home first and inform his parents of his duty to the king. "I'll be back shortly." He kissed her lightly on the cheek and then mounted his horse and rode off at a gallop. She watched from the window as he disappeared down the driveway. Tonight we shall be alone at last she thought to herself.

Doctor John listened as Jonathan told him about the king and his request for Jonathan to assist the royal doctors. "Be careful son, let the king's doctors do the examination, if anything goes wrong they will put the blame on you, be cautious." Jonathan said he would probably be staying at Boughey Hall for a while. Lord Fairbanks was away on his business so he would be added company for Lady Patricia. Mrs Godwin looked at Jonathan. "Remember your place son, Lady Patricia will have to marry a nobleman, Lord Fairbanks is adamant about that."

The two doctors looked up as Doctor Jonathan entered the room. "Ah! Now we can begin," said Captain Howard.

The collar supporting the king's neck was removed carefully. His majesty was awake but didn't look very happy. The doctor asked if he could move his head. Jonathan suggested he put his hand under the neck to add a little support. Captain Howard stood aside and asked Jonathan if he would like to do it. Gently, his hand moved into position and Jonathan asked the king to try turning his head, first one way and then the other. The king obliged, Jonathan could feel the neck muscles working. He let his hand investigate further. There was still some swelling but the king did not complain as he carried out the manoeuvre. He addressed the two doctors. "It does not appear to be a broken neck, just a badly bruised one. There still is some swelling that needs some attention but so far so good. I think a soft collar would help his majesty instead of that hard one. He should be encouraged to move his head now but only a little at a time and if any anti-inflammatory cream is available a little application should help. I would also suggest that we leave it at that for today gentlemen. Let's proceed slowly and with caution." Jonathan looked at the king and smiled. "Well done, Sire." The two doctors moved in and started talking to the king in hushed tones.

rd Samuel Hagleigh stood proudly in front of the
his uniform had been made to measure, and he looked
⎯⎯hart. His acceptance into the artillery brigade went
smoothly and of course, his title automatically meant officer
status. He was being trained as a commander of the cannon
company and would be spending many hours on the ranges.
His crippled hand didn't hold him back in his new career.
Lieutenant Hagleigh was once again a happy man. Before the
training began, Captain Blaine suggested a weekend in
London, some relaxation and fun, so they made their way into
the city. Samuel had written to his parents but had not
received any reply.

Dick Turpin and John King prowled the streets looking
for opportunities as they referred to it. Anybody showing
wealth was their victim. They often sat in taverns frequented
by travellers and would often converse with potential victims
finding out their businesses and would then follow them, and
when they had cleared the city limits the gang would strike
and rob them.

Captain Blaine and Lieutenant Hagleigh also frequented
the taverns on their weekend of fun and frivolity and it was
inevitable that at some time the Turpin and King duo would
cross paths.

Lieutenant Hagleigh sat with his back to the door as
Turpin and King entered, and did not notice them. It was only
after a bawdy crowd started to get noisy as the Lieutenant
turned around. His eyes fell on the two men who were just
leaving. The first man was a stranger but the second man had
a touch of familiarity about him. The Lieutenant left his seat
and rushed to the door for a better look. The two men were
just mingling with the crown but the Lieutenant recognised

the man who had put a bullet through his sword hand. Captain Blaine asked what was the problem. They left the tavern in pursuit but the crowd had swallowed them up.

Captain Howard greeted Lady Patricia and Jonathan as they entered the king's bedroom. He had been on duty half the night and now it was Jonathan's turn to stay at the king's bedside until Captain Perrie took over. The king had slept peacefully all night it was time to wake him for his breakfast. Lady Patricia seated herself at the side of the bed and spoke quietly to the king. She held his hand and stroked his brow. "Your majesty it is time for breakfast, are you awake, Sire?"

His eyes flickered and then opened. "Yes, my dear, I am awake now." Jonathan greeted his majesty and enquired of this well being. "Ah! Doctor Jonathan, I have had a comfortable night thanks to you, are you going to be treating me some more today?" Jonathan said that after breakfast he would further examine his majesty. They managed to raise the king's shoulders and supported him with pillows. The food was more solids now, cereals instead of soups and the king managed to swallow alright. "Has the coach arrived from London yet?" he asked. "I've heard them talking about it." Jonathan said he hadn't seen it or heard anyone mention it. Lady Patricia finished feeding the king and moved away. Jonathan immediately began to feel around the king's neck. The swelling had gone down more and Jonathan began to feel down the spine. He helped the king into a sitting position and continued to run his fingers further down the spine. The king winced a couple of times as Jonathan probed. He lay the king down again. "There's a problem your majesty which needs some careful treatment. Your spine is slightly out of line, this will have to be carefully manipulated and gently massaged. It needs expert handling. I hope your surgeons are capable of doing it." The king looked at Jonathan. "You will inform them of your findings, Doctor and find out if they are capable."

Captain Perrie entered the room and greeted the king and Jonathan. "The coach should arrive today from London. We have decided that tomorrow we will be taking his majesty home where we can begin treatment." He smiled at Jonathan. "Thank you for your help, Doctor, I'm sure his majesty appreciates all that you have done for him." Jonathan took the doctor to one side. "His spine is out of line and very tender, he will need special treatment. There could even be more serious injuries lower down. Do you have anyone with experience of spinal injuries doctor?" Captain Perrie said that there were all kinds of specialists at the king's beckoning and he felt sure one they get back to London the king would be in the best of care.

Lady Patricia entered the room with the two orderlies who kept his majesty clean and tidy. "Be careful with his back, Jonathan advised them." Patricia said the king's coach had arrived. Jonathan said he would go down and take a look. Captain Howard and Captain Perrie, the king's surgeons were already inspecting the coach. It had been fitted out with a bed and a seat on either side for the two doctors. Jonathan got inside and felt the mattress. He didn't think it was firm enough or hard enough. He asked the two doctors if more padding could be added and also a board under the mattress. They were undecided and thought it was adequate as it was. Jonathan insisted it needed more attention. "The king has to lie on that for a very rough journey, it will be you who faces the consequences if the king suffers. I have made my recommendations, now it is up to you." Jonathan walked away; he had upset the doctors again.

Lady Patricia was in the king's bedroom and the orderlies had finished. "We need to find the king some warm clothing for travelling. I think they will be leaving today."

The king was awake. "Sire, the coach has arrived, I believe you will be leaving us today." Jonathan sat at the side of the bed. "Am I going to be alright, Doctor Jonathan?" the king asked.

"If they take it easy and avoid the bumps I'm sure you will arrive safely in London, Sire. I just wish you had been staying here longer, I would have liked to see you walking again."

The king reached for Jonathan's hand. "I owe you everything, Doctor. I shall not forget you and your Lady Patricia."

Jonathan allowed the king's physicians to supervise his transportation. Lady Patricia had dressed him in some warm gowns and provided blankets. They watched as the coach left under armed escort. Lord Fairbanks returned just in time to see his important guests' departure.

Everything returned to normal after a few days. Jonathan returned home and began looking after his patients.

Chapter 6

The convent was Jonathan's first call and Mother Superior greeted him in the hallway leading to the ward. She was very pleased with the way the patients were responding especially the soldier who was almost back to this normal self. Jonathan examined him thoroughly and said that in one week's time he will discharge him. He next looked in on the gipsy girl who was sitting up in bed looking quite perky. Jonathan examined her thoroughly. There was a vast improvement, just a hint of a cough but her chest sounded well. He informed the nuns to carry on with the treatment. Lady Bingley's daughter also showed signs of improvement and Jonathan suggested keeping up the treatment. The ones who hadn't been getting the special treatment seemed stable enough but still slightly under the weather. Jonathan instructed the nuns to treat them the same as the soldier had been treated. The cream to be rubbed on their chest and back twice a day and a spoonful of rosehip syrup three times a day and to put joss sticks around the room to sweeten the air. He forecast that within two weeks all would be going home cured.

His next call was to the monastery to see Brother Thomas. He needed more of the cream and the syrup and of course his specially prepared joss sticks.

He was greeted by a very happy monk who had just received a consignment of various herbs and other concoctions from his contact in China. The goods had taken a while to reach him due to the problems with the shipping, naval activity certainly made shipping goods by sea difficult. Jonathan told Brother Thomas that his medicines had been very beneficial in treating the chest infections at the monastery. Brother Thomas said he was very pleased and offered the doctor a drink from his selection. The nettle wine tasted beautiful and Jonathan accepted a refill. Brother Thomas asked Jonathan if he could pick up some more glassware from the glassmakers. Jonathan was looking at the skeleton again and showing great interest. Brother Thomas took it down and laid it on the table. "What is it, Doctor Jonathan?" he asked. Jonathan fiddled about with the bony structure. "If the spine becomes misaligned through some kind of fall, what would be the best way to realign it?" Brother Thomas began manipulating it from the neck downwards. "Gently massage the spine and just pulling slightly feeling the structure and gently manipulating but only a little at a time." Jonathan asked how long to work all the way down. Brother Thomas said it depended on how painful the patient found it, sometimes by pulling gently on the legs the spine may realign itself but it is a very delicate process. If not done correctly, the patient could become paralysed for life.

Jonathan thanked the monk and said he would call again with the glassware. His next place to visit was the Western Towers. The builders had finished ahead of schedule and Doctor John had asked his son to join him and his mother on a final inspection. They were gathered in the hallway where the reception area had been set up, the architect proudly showing them around. There were doors leading off to various other rooms; a consulting room, a large dispensary which had yet to be stocked up with available medicines and a waiting room. A staff room where the nurses would be working and a ground floor toilet area.

The architect led them up the wide staircase, which hadn't been altered, onto the first floor. Wooden painted signs indicated which ward was where. They were shown into each room which was tastefully furnished and had views from the windows overlooking the gardens and the river. The second floor was very much the same with occasional rooms allocated to the nursing staff who would provide a 24 hour duty. Jonathan was impressed. His mother asked if there were facilities for nurse training which would be her priority. The architect looked at his plans and pointed to a room on the ground floor at the rear of the building.

Captain Blaine had assured Lieutenant Hagleigh that after they had finished their training on the ranges they would trawl the streets of London looking for the man Samuel had seen but for the next few weeks, their time would be spent on the cannon range preparing the artillery for any ensuing battles with the French. Turpin was unaware that he had been spotted, it was the furthest thing from his mind as the Essex gang carried out their robbery sprees.

After the conducted tour, Jonathan made his apologies and left. He wanted to see Patricia. He made his way to Boughey Hall now absent of the military who had been marched back to the ranges on Cank Thorn. He noticed that Lord Fairbanks' coach had returned and was in the coach house being washed and cleaned. Marston the butler showed

Jonathan into the library. "I'll inform her ladyship of your arrival, Doctor, she is with Lord Fairbanks at the moment."

It was ten minutes before she entered the library smiling at Jonathan and giving him a hug. "Uncle arrived in time to see the king on his way and to be able to hand over the taxes. That will save my uncle a journey to London. He is tired now and his gout is playing him up. Can you ask your father to pay him a visit?"

Mrs Godwin had recruited four possible women to be trained as nurses. They were waiting for the surgery to begin. The first thing Mrs Godwin made them do was to scrub their hands in the sink. "Cleanliness is everything," she said examining them, and of course, you will wear an apron which we will provide. She chose one of the women to be a patient. "Now we will begin by dressing wounds." She drew a big line on the patient's leg. "This woman has fallen and caught her leg on a piece of rusty iron. First we will clean the wound thoroughly."

Doctor John had already gone on his rounds and Jonathan was busying himself with paperwork and compiling a list of medicines to be handed into the apothecary in the town. He could hear his mother giving instructions in the surgery, he smiled to himself, she was in her element, just the person to be in charge of nursing at Western Towers.

Doctor John was visiting two of the gentry on the outskirts of the town but decided to call in to see Lord Hagleigh on his way. He was shown into the library where Lord Hagleigh was scrutinising a letter from his son Lieutenant Samuel Hagleigh. He greeted Doctor John courteously before exploding into a foul mood. "He's gone and joined the military," he blurted out, "of all the stupid things to do." Doctor John asked to whom he was referring. "Samuel, my eldest son, he's training to be an artillery commander, the stupid man. He had everything here, a good business to run, what on earth possessed him to volunteer for the military." Doctor John listened as Lord Hagleigh rambled on. "I think possibly, my lord, this may be a good thing for Lord Samuel, it will help lift him out of his depression, and change will do him good." Lord Hagleigh calmed down and offered the doctor a glass of wine. The subject then changed and Lord Hagleigh asked about the Western tower infirmary. He said it was most impressive and complimented the doctor on his achievement. Doctor John said he hoped it would be a success and hoped one day a similar venture for poorer classes could be funded.

Mrs Godwin dismissed the class. It was almost lunchtime. The women were told to attend the next class in two days time.

Doctor Jonathan said he would be going out after lunch. He said his father had promised to call on Lord Fairbanks that day and didn't anticipate him making it for lunch as his lordship was feeling a bit grumpy with his gout playing up. "They will probably be playing cards for quite a while; it's the only thing that puts his lordship in a good mood especially if he wins."

After lunch, Jonathan asked Edward to saddle his horse. "I'm off to the glassworks and then to the Priory and then to the convent."

"Shall you not be visiting Lady Patricia?" his mother enquired.

"Maybe, Mother, if I have the time," said Jonathan, "it's been almost a week and maybe I can rescue Father from Lord Fairbanks if he's still there."

Chapter 7

The king was in a foul mood, his doctors had just visited him and had examined his broken leg; they hadn't been very gentle and now his whole body was wrecked with pain. Lord Percival and Lord Hastings hurried along the corridors to the king's chambers. "He's still in a lot of pain," said Lord Percival, "I know the journey didn't go as smoothly as we anticipated; all those potholes in the roads. The coachman couldn't see them in the dark; I wish we had stayed at Boughey hall a little longer."

They entered the king's bedroom; his servants had just finished washing and cleaning him. He was now half sitting up supported by lots of pillows. He scowled at the two lords as they greeted him with "Good morning, your majesty". The affairs of the day still had to be dealt with and important papers to be signed. There was a list of people who wanted an audience with the king. There were also military matters to be discussed.

"When am I going to be well enough to deal with all these affairs of the state?" The king moaned.

His advisers shook their heads. "You are not well enough yet, your majesty, that was a nasty accident you had and it has only been just over a month, your surgeons are doing all they can to get you back on your feet."

The king shouted at them, "Why didn't you leave me a while longer at Boughey hall with Lord Fairbanks, that young Doctor Jonathan Godwin was doing more than the two halfwits I have looking after me. They won't even tell me if I am going to be able to walk again. I want that young doctor to treat me. Send for him." Lord Percival said he didn't know if the young doctor was available. The king scowled at him, "I will write to Lord Fairbanks, he will ask the doctor, get me something to write with and a courier."

Lord Hastings left the king's chamber and hurriedly found writing materials. He found the king's doctors and asked what they were doing for the king. Captain Howard said the king was too impatient; they still hadn't been able to examine his back yet. The journey had shaken him up and they needed to wait until things had settled down again. Captain Howard said we were thinking of having a special chair made which could be moved around. If the king was more mobile, perhaps he would be a little more pleasant. Lord Hastings waved the writing paper at them. "He's sending for that young Doctor Godwin, he wants him to treat him." The doctors looked at him amazed. "Well, let him, the responsibility will be out of our hands then."

Lord Fairbanks retreated to the drawing room where the butler brought his glass of wine. "There's a courier from the royal palace just arrived, my lord, with an urgent letter. Shall I show him in?"

Lord Fairbanks looked surprised. "Yes certainly, I wonder what that is all about."

The courier handed over the letter bearing the king's seal. Lord Fairbanks instructed the butler to see that the messenger received food and drink. When he was alone, he opened the letter from the king. When he had read the contents, he rang the bell for the butler. "Marston, I want to send a letter to Doctor Jonathan Godwin, will you arrange for someone to take it at once, it's very urgent." Lord Fairbanks quickly scribbled a note and popped it in an envelope and sealed it. "There, Marston, if you would get that delivered straight away."

Lady Patricia joined her uncle in the drawing room asking him if all was well. He seemed to be in a better mood now after Doctor John's visit. "Did you win at cards, Uncle?" she asked smiling at him.

"I've got some news to tell you, Patricia, some good and some bad."

She giggled excitedly. "Go on then, Uncle, tell me please."

He made her sit next to him. "Well, the good news is Lord Samuel Hagleigh has joined the military so you won't see him for a while. The bad news is the king wants Doctor Jonathan to go to the palace for an audience with him. I don't know what for but he wants him to go right away." Patricia looked puzzled. "I wonder what he wants Jonathan for."

Jonathan read Lord Fairbanks letter and told Edward not to stable his horse. "I've got to go out again," he told his mother, "I'm going to Boughey Hall after all."

Mrs Godwin addressed her son, "Well, if your father is still there tell him he's missed his lunch."

Jonathan rode across the fields; it was unusual for Lord Fairbanks to summon him, after all, his father had visited him that day so it couldn't be anything health wise. Marston answered the door and showed Jonathan into the drawing room where Lord Fairbanks and Patricia were taking afternoon tea. "Ah! Doctor Jonathan, you will be wondering why I have summoned you, please sit down." He handed Jonathan the king's letter. "A special request for you to attend an audience with his majesty."

Jonathan read the letter, looked at Lord Fairbanks and Patricia. "I wonder what he wants," said a surprised Jonathan.

"Probably to thank you for looking after him," said Patricia, "let's have a glass of uncle's special wine to celebrate, Oh, and another surprise, Lord Samuel Hagleigh has enlisted in the military."

Mrs Godwin greeted her husband and asked if he had seen Jonathan. He looked through the window and said, "He's just arrived, my dear, now we can all sit down for our evening meal." Jonathan greeted them both with a huge smile on his face.

"Why are you so excited?" asked his father. When they were all seated around the table he showed them Lord Fairbanks letter. "Well, I never thought I would see the day when my son was invited to the palace by the king of England," Doctor John added, "that's not surprising, my dear, you have just had the king staying here and you have even washed him personally." Doctor John addressed Jonathan, "Did Lord Fairbanks tell you about Lord Hagleigh joining the military?" Jonathan nodded. "Yes, Father and that's also good news."

The London coach left from Lichfield on Saturdays and Doctor and Mrs Godwin drove the carriage to the Three Tunns Tavern where Jonathan boarded. He bade farewell to his parents saying he would write to them soon. He settled down with the other passengers for what would be a long journey staying overnight in Northampton.

Mrs Godwin prepared the surgery for the next day's training session. She had now recruited a total of six, which would be enough to start with. She had also taken it on herself to select the cleaners and chambermaids so she had a busy work schedule on her hands. Doctor John looked after patients who had booked in at the surgery.

Sir James Godfrey had his whole company on parade ready to meet the new contingency marching up from London. He was pleased with the results of the first company, all were now qualified marksmen. Two hundred highly trained soldiers were ready for battle with the French if they asked for it. Captain Marshall called the company to attention as the new company entered the forest and marched smartly to the ranges.

Dick Turpin lay on his back. It's a pity things went wrong on his visit to Stafford, Jack Slade had confided in him regarding the king's tax collector who had made his rounds collecting taxes from the noble gentry every three months and collected quite a large sum of money. "Perhaps, I'll go back one day," he murmured to himself.

Doctor John called in at the convent, Jonathan had told him that the soldier was fit enough to be released in time to march to London with his company. Mother Superior greeted him and escorted him to the isolation ward. The soldier was up and helping the nuns. Doctor John gave him a final examination and told him he was fit to return to his company.

It was a four-mile walk back to the rangers but he was glad to make it.

Mother Superior escorted the doctor around the ward. The gipsy girl and Lady Brindley's daughter had responded to the treatment and were well on their way to a full recovery.

Doctor John addressed the nun, "Thank goodness, it was just a bad chest infection and nothing more serious as we first thought. Carry on treating all the patients the same and I can foresee them all being discharged shortly."

His next visit was to Western Towers. The medicines had arrived and were locked away in the dispensary. Reception staff had been recruited and trained and also orderlies to make themselves useful wherever they were needed. Doctor John now wanted to arrange an official opening day and a plaque put on the wall to commemorate the occasion. Lord Hagleigh had donated 20 tons of fine aggregate to smarten up the driveway to the infirmary.

Jonathan relaxed and enjoyed light conversations with fellow travellers. A short distance from Lichfield the coachman announced that one of the horses had developed a slight limp. They would have to call to a coaching inn and change horses. It was only a short stop but the passengers were able to stretch their legs. Jonathan called into the bar for a glass of water. He started chatting to the innkeeper who pointed out that this was only a temporary post for him until a new tenant could be found. Jonathan liked the warm feel of the place and said he might consider an investment. He liked the name of the inn 'The Highwayman'.

Back on the coach, they were soon back on the London road enjoying the scenery. A stopover for lunch and another exchange of horses in Northampton saw some passengers departing and others taking their places. It seemed a long journey to Jonathan but he took it in his stride. His mind was preoccupied with what was the purpose of his royal invitation. He had only visited London once years ago during his medical training. It was a bustling place and Jonathan was a bit concerned as to whether he could find his way around. The coach finally stopped outside a large coaching station which appeared to be the terminus. The coachman unloaded the luggage onto the pavement. Jonathan asked if he could direct him to the palace. Pointing his finger to a large building in the distance flying flags from its tower the man told Jonathan to head in that direction. He found that London was a vibrant city but not to his liking, all the hustle and bustle and everyone seemed to be in a rush. Jonathan preferred to be in the countryside, the small market towns appealed to him more so. He made his way through the busy streets towards the palace, again trying not to bump into the throngs of people massing around the palace gates. Coaches weaved in and out, the more luxury looking ones bearing elegantly dressed passengers; passengers were hell-bent on passing through the heavily guarded gates. Jonathan was approached by an important looking officer of the guard who demanded to know where Jonathan was going. Showing him the letter sent to him by the palace, he was escorted through a narrow gate to a building inside the grounds. His letter was scrutinised by an official-looking gentleman who told him to wait. A few moments lapsed before another gentleman appeared and told Jonathan to follow him. He was led through long corridors into the heart of the palace where another gentleman was waiting to receive him. His letter was handed back to him and he was again led through more long corridors and handed over to another well-dressed gentleman who introduced himself as Lord Ashcroft, secretary to the royal household. He told Jonathan that the king had been informed of his arrival but today was a busy day and Jonathan was at the end of a long queue of courtiers, all of whom had appointments to see the king. Jonathan felt slightly underdressed amongst the gentlemen dressed in all their finery. He was asked to take a seat and wait until he was summonsed.

Barely two hours had passed before he was approached by an elderly gentleman who asked Jonathan for his letter. Scrutinising the contents he indicated for Jonathan to follow him. Much to the concern of the other waiting gentlemen, he was led to the front of the queue and into a small side room where another gentleman was waiting. This time he was greeted more courteously and told that the king had expressed his sincere apologies for keeping Jonathan waiting. Another door opened and he was led into a large room luxuriously furnished. Jonathan could see someone sitting in a very large and well-upholstered reclining chair by a very large window the door closed behind him. Jonathan approached slowly not quite knowing what to do. The man sitting in the chair beckoned him forward. "Doctor Jonathan, I am so pleased to see you again." Jonathan recognised the voice at once and bowed. "Your majesty, I am honoured to be here, how are you?"

At a glance, he could see the pain etched into the king's face. He was not sitting very comfortably and every movement was painful. "As you can see, my dear doctor, I have not greatly improved since we parted. I still can hardly move and I am confined to this contraption so that they can push me around the palace, it is a nightmare, Doctor. Those so-called doctors of mine don't know what to do, that's why I have sent for you to see if you can help me more. You have skills my doctors don't know about. Will you stay and help me to get better?" Jonathan looked at the king; he was pleading with him for his help. How could he refuse to help his monarch but first there would have to be a 100% examination without any interference from the royal doctors. "Sire, I will help you with all I can but first I see you have a busy work schedule ahead of you and I must find some form of accommodation for myself."

The king raised his hands. "Doctor Jonathan, you will be accommodated here in the palace next to my private quarters and all your needs attended to by my servants. As for my working schedule, I will finish what I have today and then my staff will see to the rest. I must admit I'm more concerned with walking again than I am with that fat Frenchman Napoleon." He pulled a cord to summon his aide. Jonathan addressed the king, "Sire, I shall want to see you in the morning after breakfast. You will remain in your night attire and I will make a full examination in private with no interference from your own medical staff and all my findings shall remain between the two of us, is that understood, Sire?" The King stretched out his hand to shake hands with Jonathan. "I have the utmost faith in you, Doctor. I can feel it in my bones and your confidence oozes from you. I will see you tomorrow morning and a new day will begin for me."

Jonathan shook the monarch's hand and followed the servant through a couple of doors leading into a small bedroom containing a table and two chairs, a medium-sized bed and a wardrobe. The servant said he would return shortly with food and drink.

Captain Blaine and Lieutenant Samuel Hagleigh trawled the streets of London, every chance they had looking and searching for the robber who had caused Lieutenant Samuel's injuries. Samuel was adamant he had seen the man leave the tavern weeks ago but had lost him. Now he was hell-bent on finding him again. Captain Blaine suggested that if they find him they would follow him and find out where he was staying and then with a few good men from their company would surprise him and arrest him, the plan was a good one but they had to find the man first.

Dick Turpin and the gang had been working outside of the city preying on travellers travelling up from the south. They had recouped much loot and now heading back to the city to have a good time. John King was the leader of the Essex Gang and ruled with a rod of iron. Dick Turpin accepted this but not always with a smile on his face. John King ordered the gang to break up and to enter the city from different directions, meeting up at their favourite water hole. They were told to keep a low profile and not to be too bawdy. He and Turpin would arrive later.

Captain Blaine and Lieutenant Samuel Hagleigh were in London for a couple of days staying at a well-known tavern used mainly by the military personnel. Their evenings were spent trawling the back street taverns. The one tavern looked familiar to Hagleigh. "'The Green Man', was that the one we were in a few weeks ago?" asked Samuel.

"Yes, I believe it is," replied Captain Blaine, "shall we go and sample their wine, I'm getting a thirst on."

They made their way to a table in a corner at the back of the tavern. The crowd of drinkers took no notice as they were being entertained by the bawdy ladies plying their favours. After an hour, Lieutenant Hagleigh suggested moving on. They managed to push their way through the crowd towards the door. Lieutenant Hagleigh chanced to look back as a noisy pair descended the stairs. The woman was all over the man as he tried to make it to a table. Samuel's eyes opened as he recognised Turpin. Captain Blaine pulled on his sleeve. "Not here, not now Samuel, let's wait for him to leave, there are too many of his friends in here we would be mobbed." Lieutenant Hagleigh smiled an evil smile. "Got you and now I'm going to kill you."

Captain Blaine managed to steer Lieutenant Hagleigh out of the tavern and into the streets. "We can't do anything here, Samuel, we will wait until he comes out and then follow him to his lodgings, then we can arrange for his arrest when we have the men with us, and we must get a warrant for his arrest, it must be done legally, Samuel."

They waited patiently for two hours concealed in the shadows opposite the tavern. Captain Blaine was almost asleep on his feet when a boisterous crowd emerged onto the streets. Lieutenant Hagleigh scrutinised the men as they left the tavern. Turpin was the last to leave unable to tear himself away from his female companion. Finally, he broke free and followed his companions. Captain Blaine and Lieutenant Hagleigh followed closely.

Doctor Jonathan had risen early; he wanted to pay the king a quick visit before leaving for home. The servant arrived with a tray of food. Jonathan asked if the king was awake and said he would like a quick audience with his majesty before his departure. The servant returned within the hour and escorted Jonathan to the king's chambers. "Good morning, Doctor Godwin, I trust you slept well." His majesty was in good humour and beckoned Jonathan to his bedside. First, the doctor examined the mattress on the king's bed. "This will have to be changed, Sire, it is not firm enough and I would like to see it replaced, also a large board must be placed underneath the firmer mattress to support your spine. I'm not surprised you are uncomfortable." Jonathan asked the king to try and roll over onto his stomach. Jonathan and the servant helped turn him over. Next, Jonathan told the king that he would lift his gown so that he could examine the king thoroughly. Starting from the base of the skull, Jonathan probed the bone structure indicating the king to let him know when the pain was relevant. Gradually, his fingers felt each part of the spinal cord, noticing any pain felt by the king. Jonathan kept his eyes closed, his mind concentrating on the king's spine. It was a lengthy examination from the neck to the small of the back and Jonathan felt many irregularities.

He moved his hands gently down the king's body until he reached his feet. Running his fingers along the sole he felt for the slight twitches he was looking for. He asked his majesty to roll over onto his back and again concentrated on the feet. After a very thorough examination, Jonathan pulled up a chair and sat at the king's side. The king was anxious to know what the doctor had discovered. He took Jonathan's hand. "Tell me, Doctor Godwin, will I ever be able to walk again?" Jonathan was writing notes in his diary. "Sire, I want you to listen carefully to what I have to say and to follow my instructions to the letter and certainly no interventions from your own doctors. Your spine is still in a very bad shape but with careful manipulations and gentle massage, I think we can rectify the problems but it will take time and a great deal of effort on your behalf, patience is required. I am now going home to get all the things I will require for your treatment and I will return in a few days. In the meantime, I want a firm table made for you to lie on, well-padded and a hole at one end for your majesty to rest your face. I need you absolutely flat on this table. Can you arrange for this to be ready on my return?" The king agreed that everything Jonathan had said would be complied with. He also insisted that his private coach would be made available for Jonathan's transportation. Jonathan gave the servant a small container with an ointment inside to be applied to the king's back morning and night. He also directed the king to stay in his bed until he returned. "No official duties to be undertaken, Sire." He said his goodbyes and departed, leaving the king in a good sense of humour.

Chapter 8

Captain Blaine showed Lieutenant Hagleigh the warrant for the arrest of Dick Turpin. He was charged with murder, robbery and wounding a nobleman. "Will that be sufficient to hang him?" asked Lieutenant Hagleigh. Captain Blaine said it would be and they could also accuse him of being a highwayman that was a hanging offence. Blaine dispersed the men into the shadows around the stable block. Turpin always visited his horse last thing at night. It had started to drizzle and a slight mist accompanied it. Captain Blaine's men huddled in the doorways where they could. Shortly before midnight, the familiar footsteps echoed on the cobblestones as Turpin made his way to the stables. Blaine waited until Turpin entered the stable before descending on the unsuspecting victim. As Turpin struggled, Lieutenant Hagleigh gave him an almighty crack on the head rendering him unconscious. "Right, tie his hands behind him and we will drag him to the palace gates where our other friends will take him from us and lock him up." Lieutenant Hagleigh smiled a wicked smile as the prisoner was bundled into the cells. "Now I'm going to see you hang."

Doctor John arrived at Western Towers well before the open day was due to start. Mrs Godwin said she wanted to take a quick look around before the visitors started pouring in.

Doctor John visited Lady Isabella and asked her to escort him into the infirmary to greet the guests. Refreshments were placed on tables for the visitors to help themselves.

Squire Brindley and his family were the first to arrive followed by other dignitaries from around the area. Doctor John and Lady Isabella greeted them as they entered the hall. Mrs Godwin had assembled her nursing staff all wearing their new uniforms, pale blue with white collars and cuffs. The architect and senior members escorted the visitors around, showing them the different rooms and other facilities available. One or two of the paid-up gentry already had family members installed in some rooms and who were already receiving treatment for various ailments.

Lord Fairbanks arrived with his niece Lady Patricia and were greeted warmly by the doctor and Mrs Godwin. Lady Patricia enquired if Doctor Jonathan had returned yet adding, "I do hope the king isn't going to steal him away from us."

Doctor Jonathan and the coach entered the large courtyard where they would stay. The coachman unharnessed the horses and stabled them. Jonathan booked the rooms and after a hearty meal retired for the night. There was something heavy in the bottom of his back that Jonathan wasn't sure about. Reaching in, he pulled out a leather purse with the royal emblem on it. Jonathan's eyes opened as the gold sovereigns poured out onto the bed. It would appear as if the king had rewarded him handsomely.

The coachman was ready and waiting when Jonathan had a light breakfast and went outside. The remaining journey didn't seem to take long. Soon Jonathan was looking at the large cathedral spires of Lichfield, he was getting excited he had missed his parents and above all Lady Patricia. They would be disappointed when he told them he was returning to London in a matter of days but it was for the King of England; he had his duty to the king, besides he liked the king and was pleased and honoured that he had been chosen.

The coach swung into the surgery courtyard and soon Doctor John and Mrs Godwin had emerged from the surgery. They were surprised to find their royal visitor was no other than their son Jonathan. He was greeted enthusiastically and spirited into the house followed by a barrage of questions from his parents. "I am only here for a few days; I have to get back to the king in London. I've only come to get my things and then I have to be off again."

The table was laid and Mrs Godwin prepared lunch. Jonathan told all that had happened and that the king wanted him to stay at the palace and treat him. Doctor John frowned. "It is a remarkable undertaking, Jonathan, do you think you are up to it?" His son looked at his father. "I can certainly do more than those royal doctors; they have no idea at all. I told his majesty I would do what I could but I gave no guarantees."

Jonathan asked Edward to saddle his horse. "I have to go and collect some things from Brother Thomas and I will call and see Lady Patricia. I also want some things from the apothecary so I will be gone for most of the day." His father informed him that the open day at the infirmary had gone well. Jonathan apologised for his absence but promised his undivided attention when he returned from London.

Jonathan greeted Brother Thomas and was immediately invited to taste his latest concoction. "A fruit juice from the wild apples growing in the forest," said Brother Thomas, "I do love searching in the forest, it's so rich in plants and herbs. Now, Jonathan, tell me what you have been up to?" Brother

Thomas listened open-mouthed as Jonathan reported all that had taken place. "I can't believe you have met the king, nevertheless been treating his injuries, and now you are his personal doctor. This was all kept hush-hush, Jonathan, no one around here has heard about it." Jonathan remarked on how tight the security had been. "Well, what can I get you now, my friend?" said Thomas. Jonathan looked at the skeleton. "I need to borrow this Thomas, as a guide when I'm working on the king's back, do you have another one I could borrow?" Thomas opened a cupboard and brought out a bag containing a lot of bones. "I have this one but it's not assembled yet, if you can help me to put it together I can wire it up for you." He laid out the bones and began putting them in their right order, he carefully thread the thin wire through each tiny hole before pulling it tight. "I'll leave the skull detached, it will travel better. Jonathan do be careful, remember how slowly you have to work feeling in between the joint very gently."

Jonathan thanked his friend and thanked him for all the tuition he had received. Now, he needed some pain relief, potions and compounds. "How long do you think it should take me to completely realign the spine using your method of manipulation and massage, Brother Thomas?" The monk thought for a while. "Take it a little at a time, do not rush, and see how the patient is responding. When all seems to be in order, plenty of gentle warm massage and after a few days, if all is well, try it in a large pool of warm water, it will ease things a lot, and also try some gentle stretching of the legs and upper body. If all seems alright, try standing the king on his feet, supported of course, and then gradually work on what you see."

Jonathan had everything he had come for. Thanking Brother Thomas, he left the monastery and made his way across the country to Boughey Hall. Lady Patricia shielded her eyes from the sun when she saw the horseman riding along the driveway. Her instinct told her it was Jonathan so she began to run, jumping into the arms of Jonathan as he got down from his horse.

"Jonathan!" Her lips brushed lightly across his cheeks before she kissed his lips.

"Patricia, I have missed you," he whispered.

"Are you here to stay, Jonathan?" she asked holding onto him?"

He smiled at her and hugged her. "No, not yet, Patricia, I have not finished treating the king, I have just come for a quick visit to get some things and then I must return to London. I'm sorry, Patricia, the king insists I treat him, his doctors are useless. I promise, as soon as I can get his majesty back on his feet I will return to you. That's my promise to you, Patricia." She cupped her arm through his and they walked around the grounds.

Lord Fairbanks hailed them through the French windows of the drawing room and Jonathan and Patricia made their way towards him. "Doctor Jonathan, so pleased to see you, is the king fully recovered from his fall?" Jonathan explained the situation to Lord Fairbanks and said, "A little more time was going to be needed and a lot of luck."

A quick meal was prepared and they sat down together exchanging pleasantries. Lord Fairbanks said the opening of the infirmary had gone down well, thanks to Doctor John and all concerned. He also asked Jonathan if he had heard anything about Lord Samuel Hagleigh or Lieutenant Samuel

Hagleigh as he is called these days. Jonathan said he hadn't heard or seen him for a long time now since we went off and joined the military. Lady Patricia escorted her uncle to his room where he would take a nap. Jonathan waited for her return, announcing that he had to be going as the coach would be leaving early the next morning. He held Patricia in his arms and kissed her fully on the lips. "You must do that more often, Jonathan," she said returning the kiss. "If only your uncle would allow it," he whispered.

The journey back to London was uneventful as light drizzle ploughed its way through grey dawn. Jonathan dosed on and off. A short break and a change of horses and soon the rest of the road opened up before them. It was early evening when they echoed through the castle courtyard. Jonathan gathered his things and made for his room. A light meal and early to bed, tomorrow was going to be a busy day.

The king's servant knocked on the door and entered on command. Placing the tray of food on the table, he asked if Jonathan had had a good journey adding that the king had rested well and was in good humour. Jonathan ate a light breakfast and then checked the contents of his luggage. The servant entered and informed the doctor that the king was ready to receive him. Jonathan knocked on the door and entered. The king was in bed with shoulders raised slightly. "I trust your majesty is comfortable," said Jonathan in response to the huge smile that greeted him.

"Doctor Jonathan, I am so pleased to see you, come closer so I may shake your hand, I am most comfortable, thanks to you."

The doctor looked at the long table in the room and examined it. "Yes, Sire, that will do fine, now I must get you on to it lying flat with your face looking through that large hole. This will allow your spine to lie very flat for me."

With the help of the king's orderlies, he was transferred to the table. Jonathan made sure the king was comfortable before he began his massaging and manipulation techniques, bones were cracking as pressure was put on them. "Everything falling into line, your majesty, that's all." Moving slowly down the body, Jonathan felt his way through the king's bony structure, pressing and massaging very gently. He applied an ointment that he had brought with him, carefully massaging it into the king's body. "That smells familiar, Doctor," said the king.

"Yes, Sire, an herb from our very own countryside, and now, sire, I want you to turn over so that I can work on your broken leg, it must be almost mended by now." Jonathan started off by holding both feet and pulling down on them, asking the king to pull back. He then ran his finger along each side, checking for any reaction. Bending the left leg, he manipulated it across the king's body, watching for any response. The right leg was still too delicate for any manipulation. Jonathan said they had done enough for the morning and would resume after lunch.

The king was placed back on his bed and Jonathan sat on a chair beside him. "How's that lovely Lady Patricia, Doctor? I bet she was glad to see you!"

Jonathan smiled. "Yes, Sire, we enjoyed each other's company, brief as it was."

The king looked at Jonathan. "She is the woman for you, Doctor. Don't give up on her." He looked away from the king, embarrassed by his own birthright. If only he had been born a nobleman, her uncle may have looked more favourably on him but not on a lowly doctor's son, with no status at all.

The servants tended to the doctor's needs placing his lunch before him. The two servants were talking between themselves quietly but Jonathan caught the name, Dick Turpin. He asked the servants to tell him the topic of their conversation. "In two day's time, a highwayman is to be hung in the castle square for killing a man and wounding a nobleman. He has been sentenced, all is arranged." Jonathan toyed with his lunch, his appetite had suddenly died. After lunch when the king had had his nap, Jonathan entered the bedroom. He told the king to remain on the bed. With the help from the servants, he raised the king's shoulders and placed many pillows to raise him up, almost into a sitting position. He asked him if he was comfortable. The king gave a smile. "Yes, Doctor, I can sit up without any pain, it's all thanks to you. I owe you a lot, Doctor, ask anything of me and it will be yours."

Jonathan looked hard at the king, dare he ask? "Can you give me a dead man, Sire?"

The king looked at Jonathan as if he had been struck by lightning. "Can you make yourself clearer, Doctor? I did not understand your request."

"In your gaol, Sire, there is a man who is sentenced to hang in two days time. He is a highwayman by the name of Dick Turpin. It is said that he killed a man and injured a nobleman. I know this highwayman, Sire, he saved my life a little while ago. The nobleman in question hired two assassins to murder me. Dick Turpin saved my life, Sire."

The king looked at Jonathan. "If this is true, Doctor, then the man's life will be spared." Jonathan related the story to the king, missing nothing out. The king rang his bell for his secretary and dictated a letter pardoning on Dick Turpin and allowing for his immediate release from gaol.

Jonathan followed the secretary along corridors and down steps. The air was dank as they entered a chamber sectioned off into separate cells. The secretary handed over the letter to Jonathan. "If you wish to do the honours, sire." The gaoler examined the letter and asked the secretary if it was genuine. "It bears the king's signature and seal, of course, it's genuine. Release the prisoner at once." Dick Turpin emerged into the light blinking. He tried to focus his eyes on the man holding the letter. A surprised look crossed his face. "Is that you, Jonathan, have you come to take me to the gallows?" The secretary stepped forward. "You are free to go, Sir, the king has granted you a pardon, I suggest you make haste and depart from London post haste." Jonathan grabbed Turpin's arm. "It's true, Dick, let's get you out of here." Turpin still suffering from shock, followed Jonathan up the stairs and along rows of corridors. "I must be dreaming, Jonathan, is this for real?"

They left the palace, Jonathan gave Turpin the document. "Don't lose this, Dick or you will be rearrested. Now let's get you to your lodgings and pick up your things and then get your horse if she's still there." Jonathan had suggested leaving London immediately by the back streets, he advised Turpin to head north and to keep going. "Start a new life, Richard, that's all I can say to you." He watched as Turpin mounted Black Bess and headed off. "Promise me one more thing, Jonathan, if anything should befall me, take care of my beautiful horse, she is only five years old, she is a wonderful animal."

Doctor John took care of the morning surgery whilst Mrs Godwin went into town; it wasn't long before she had returned. A light shower had dampened everywhere and many of the shoppers had scurried to their homes. "Are you going out this afternoon?" she asked Doctor John. He looked out of the window at the weather. "No, I don't think so, I'll pop and see Lord Hagleigh and Lord Fairbanks tomorrow on my way to the infirmary."

Brother Thomas gazed at the skeleton hanging in the cupboard, he was thinking of Doctor Jonathan and his royal patient. If things went wrong and the king became crippled for life, it wouldn't look too rosy for Jonathan.

The king had finished his lunch and had had a nap. He was in good spirits and he had given Doctor Jonathan something in return. He looked across the room as Jonathan entered. "What have you got in store for me today, Doctor, not too much pain, I hope?" Jonathan stood at the bottom of the bed looking at his patient. "No pain, Sire, just some gentle manipulation, I'm going to stretch your legs today." He felt the sides of the king's feet, they were warm so the blood was flowing, which was always a good sign. Holding on to the ankles, he pulled gently, telling the king to pull against him. He manipulated each foot in different directions, feeling for any resistance from the king. He then bent both legs and tapped the knees; he noticed that the king had straightened out his right leg without any instructions from the doctor. "I see you can move that leg now, Sire; that is a good sign, now we can concentrate on that one also."

Captain Blaine hurried around the camp looking for Lieutenant Hagleigh. "Samuel, bad news I'm afraid, we've been ordered to France right away. The equipment has to be loaded up right away." Lieutenant Hagleigh uttered a round of abusive language. "Let me just stay two more days to see that man hang." Captain Blaine shook his head. "Sorry, Samuel, we start loading the canons right away, orders from the top."

The camp became a hive of activity as horse-drawn cannons lined up for despatch to the coast. "Something big coming up, Samuel, I think, we have to form an offensive front to hold Napoleon's troops from taking over the borders. We have orders to move to the coast and start boarding our ships ready to sail to France."

The king's secretary knocked on the door and the king called him in. "What is it?" he asked. The secretary bowed and walked over to the bed. Jonathan eased off a little so that the men could talk. "Good," said the king, "keep me informed of the progress. I shall hold a meeting tomorrow if the good doctor can spare me for a short while." Jonathan nodded his head. "Certainly, your majesty, I can allow you a one hour break during the morning session."

"Right, your majesty, I want you to sit on the edge of your bed and dangle your legs over the edge. Now hold onto me and try and lift your left leg." The king did as he was told and tried to lift his leg. He managed to lift a little. "Good, now the other one," said Jonathan, "this is the one that was damaged, let's see what you can do with it." The king pulled a face as he tried to lift his leg. "Go on, try a little harder, your majesty, you can do it, just a little pain." Jonathan felt the king digging in his fingers as he made the effort. "Well done, Sire, that's a start at least, it's just a matter of time and I'm sure we shall have you walking again." The king grabbed Jonathan's hand. "If you can do that for me, I'll give you anything you ask."

The cannons were lined up on the battlefield as they arrived, each section designated to a commander. Captain Blaine called to Lieutenant Hagleigh to take place on his left with his ten cannons spaced out level with his own battery.

"Try and keep level with me, Samuel, we will work as a team advancing forward after each salvo and don't forget we are firing over the heads of our specially trained riflemen, we don't want any of our own men hurt."

The artillery commanders manned their batteries waiting for orders from their higher ranking generals who were scanning the horizon through their telescopes. There was tension in the air as the morning air started to clear of the early mist. Napoleon's army was out there somewhere spying on them. "Who was going to get off the first shot" that's what everyone was saying.

Suddenly, a row of banners and flags appeared on the horizon. The enemy was lining up their artillery. Captain Blaine said they were too far away to reach their cannons. "They're not as good as ours. Let's open up on them now." The generals were huddled together discussing tactics, suddenly, word of command was given for one battery to open up and test the range. A slight elevation was adjusted and a second salvo found its mark and obliterated a couple of canons. The enemy returned fire but fell short of its target. Arrangements were made by the French to move their canons forward a bit.

Chapter 9

Dick Turpin arrived in York and found a cheap tavern to stay at and a stable for Bess. He bought some new clothes for himself with his takings and flaunted himself around the city making new friends and female acquaintances. 'A gentleman of leisure', he portrayed himself to any questions asked, and he would spend much time riding Bess across the moors looking for little insignificant places to while away the hours. Planning was his main obsession. Which way the travellers went, how often they went by coach or solitary horseback. This was his way of life, a highwayman of note, depriving others of their wealth and not having to work for it. A chancy business that had its risks but he did love the thrill of the chase. He had heard about the king's tax collector during his rounds every six months and he wanted to cash in on it, why not, the king hadn't earned it anyway.

Jonathan greeted the king after he had had his breakfast and his majesty had washed and done his ablutions. He seemed to be in a good mood as Jonathan entered his bedroom. "Good morning, Doctor, what am I in for today?" he asked the doctor cheerfully.

"Well, let's see, I've been treating you for almost six weeks now, so let's see if your legs will support your weight, Sire, I want you to sit on the edge of your bed with both feet on the floor. Now hold onto my arms and push down on your feet and try and stand up." Jonathan held tightly onto the king and helped him to his feet. "There you are, Sire, well done, now sit down again, I want you to try again now, ready?" Again, the king rose to his feet, a huge smile on his face, Jonathan let go of his arms and let the king stand alone. "There, your majesty, you are well on the way to recovery."

The king sat down again. "Soon I will be walking again, Doctor, I have you to thank for this." Jonathan asked the king to lie on the specially made bed. "Now for some gentle massaging to get the blood flowing." Jonathan asked if there were any 'spas' around the area they could get access to. The king rang his bell for his secretary and put the question to him. "I will make enquiries, your majesty. I'm sure the nobles will know if there is." Jonathan let the king rest and departed to his room where he had started to write a letter to Lady Patricia, to him, it seemed unfair as Lord Fairbanks had dictated to her that it was expected of her to marry someone of high status. He was more interested in the future of Boughey Hall. Lady Patricia was the sole benefactor and must marry someone who can afford to keep her and Boughey Hall in the family. Jonathan felt depressed, there was no way he could fit into her life although he knew that the feelings between them were right for a happy marriage.

Another week of exercise and massage followed. The king was getting stronger and now it was time to get him walking. The secretary had come up with one of the noblemen who had his own private spa at his luxurious mansion in Essex. The king had made a request for its use for two weeks with food and accommodation thrown in for the privilege of having the king of England visit him. Jonathan packed all the things he needed into the coach and with the king and a small ensemble they discreetly left the palace for Essex.

John King was livid when he heard of Turpin's pardon. Why hadn't he come back to his friends at the tavern? He made intense enquiries as to where Turpin had gone to. When word reached him that he had headed north. King was determined to follow; he wanted a share of what Turpin was after, the king's tax collector. With two men, he headed up the north road in pursuit of Turpin. Three days brought them into the heart of the city. Despatching his two men, they began searching. Turpin had taken up with a widowed shepherdess on the moors and was enjoying the privileges at her rented cottage.

King made enquiries around the city, mostly in the sleazy taverns dotted around. A week revealed no information so he concentrated on the stables and fettlers. At last on the edge of the city they found one fettler who remembered shoeing Black Bess. "A fine-looking mare if ever I saw one," he commented. King pressed him further for information. "Living out on the moors I believe. I see him pass this way sometimes." King pressed a couple of coins into his hands. "If you see him, come and let me know. I will reward you handsomely for your discretion."

The Essex gang returned to the inner city limits and booked into a cheap tavern and waited. Days passed by and the gang became restless. "Let's take a ride over the moors," said King, "Turpin may have moved on from here." They rode out to the city limits scouring different areas and asking questions. They came upon the fettler who had spoken to them previously. "No, ain't seen 'im but there's someone who rides over the moors every day exercising his horse. It may be 'im but 'e don't come near enough for me to see 'im properly." He gave them directions and they rode off. They rode a few miles before dismounting on a high knoll where they could view the moors. King scoured the land with his telescope but saw nothing. The men took it in turns looking out whilst King dozed off. Half an hour passed before he was woken by an excited shout from his man with the telescope. "There's someone coming this way John but I can't see clear enough who it be." King grabbed the telescope and told the men to hide themselves and the horses. He adjusted the scope and focused on the rider who was yet quite a long way off. The horse was black, that's all he could see. The rider had now veered off into another direction. King called the men to bring the horses; they were going to follow the man at a distance. A slight mist had already descended on the moor and the light was beginning to fail. King cursed the dawn weather and headed off after the rider. They headed in the same direction but were gradually losing visibility. They came upon a cart track that looked as if it was used frequently. They followed it cautiously until the grey shape of a building loomed in front. Not knowing if it was occupied, King decided to fall back and approach it from another direction. A slight breeze drifted across the moors, gradually clearing away with the mist. They climbed a knoll and viewed the building from a safe distance using the telescope. As far as they could make out the building was being lived in and there were sheep all around. King scanned the area. There were no people to be seen but washed clothes hanging on the line was a tell-tale sign of habitation. They lay low for a while, a door opened at the rear of the building and a man appeared leading his horse from the lean-to stable; a black horse. King trained the scope onto the man, holding his breathy to try and keep the glass focused on the man leading the horse. "If only he would walk around the other side of the horse." Breathed King. Patience persevered and the man walked the horse around. King smiled to himself. "Got you, Turpin."

The man led the horse into a small coral occupied by a mule, and let her go, it was obvious they were used to each other's company. King kept the telescope glued on the man, who simply looked around and went back into the cottage. "Right," said King to his men, looking well-pleased with himself. "We've found our man." They remained hidden until the mist started rolling in again. "Right lads, we move in closer and take a look-see." King was pleased with himself. "It'll be getting dark soon and this mist will help us, I want to get up close to the building and make sure it's im and to see who's he got with im." They moved slowly, keeping the coral between themselves and the cottage. They tied up their horses and crept forward while the two men remained by the coral. King crept forward to the front of the property, two windows illuminated by candles greeted him and the curtains were still open. King slowly manoeuvred himself to the nearest window. Turpin sat on a chair by the fire whilst a woman was preparing food on a table. "Got you, my beauties," he exclaimed, closing the telescope, he moved back to his men.

"Right, it is him and he's only got a woman with him. We'll move up closer, I and Bill go in the front door, Jack, you go in the backdoor. Don't shoot him, he can't tell us anything if he's dead." They moved into position, pistols primed and cocked ready. Dick was seated at the table with his back to the door. Nell had just started serving. King prepared himself and launched his full body weight against

144

the door. It gave way and he stood holding his pistol at the head of a surprised Dick Turpin. Nell screamed as Jack pushed through the back door. "Well, blow me if it aint our old mate Dick Turpin," scoffed King, holding the pistol to Dick's head. "What you doing 'ere matey, I thought you'd be swinging from the gallows in London. Must have friends in high places eh! Dick, why didn't you come and see your old mates before you scarpered up north. Oh! I see you were keeping the king's taxes for yourself eh! Didn't want to share with your old mates?" King swung his fist knocking Turpin to the floor. "Come on then, Dick, tell us what you've got planned for the tax collector?"

Turpin wiped the blood from his lips and got to his feet. "There's nothing planned, John, it's a no go."

King pushed Turpin back into the chair. "I know you better than that, Dick, when you're full of beer, you rattle like hell." He eyed Nell who stood there shaking. "Maybe your pretty woman here knows something." He grabbed Nell and pushed her into the bedroom. "Keep an eye on im a bit while I question er."

A fist caught Nell full in the face which knocked her onto the bed. She screamed as King abused her. "She knows nothing," Turpin blurted out. The two men pointed their pistols at him warning him not to move. They could hear Nell crying in the next room. Turpin knew how brutal King could be. "Alright, leave her alone, I'll tell you what I had planned," shouted Turpin. King got off Nell and adjusted his clothing, Nell's face was bloodied and tear-stained, she cried out in pain as King left the room. "Nice and sweet she was," crowed King.

"Right then, Dick, let's have the details," he said sitting at the table opposite Turpin. Nell gently pushed the door with her foot as she did her best to tidy herself up. Her clothes had all been torn but she managed to cover herself up a bit. The backdoor was hanging off its hinges as she crept outside. With bated breath, she crossed over to the coral, grabbing the mules' reins she crept out of the coral leading the mule. She managed to mount and steer the animal away, looking back, she saw the three horses tied to the fencing. As an afterthought, she rode back and undid the bridles, setting the horses free before she dug her heels in and rode to the city.

Turpin tried to hold their attention as he babbled on about the tax collector's round at the end of the sixth month of every year. Taxes paid to the king by every noble and farmer in the area from Staffordshire to Yorkshire, collected by one man and two servants, all together in one coach. "They're for the taking," said Turpin.

King told jack to check on the woman. "She's gone," he shouted, "slipped out the backdoor she has."

King cursed loudly. "I didn't hit her hard enough." But Nell had ridden across the moors on her mule and knew all the back trails to the city tunnels, and she also knew where to find the law.

King eyed Turpin. "Let's make some plans then, Dick, draw some maps and write down times and places."

Nell burst into the tavern where the city law enforcers hung out and ran to their table babbling hysterically. After calming her down, they listened to her story. Ten law enforcers met outside the tavern, saddled and armed. The order was given and they rode off into the night, heading for the moors.

Turpin knew that once King had the information, he would be disposed of. He was glad Nell had got away; she was probably hiding out on the moors waiting to see what happened. King was watching him closely, there was no chance he could get the better of all three of them. He drew the map slowly dragging out the times and giving King wrong instructions.

As the law enforcers neared the cottage, they were halted and dismounted. There was a light coming from the cottage but there were no horses tethered anywhere. Slowly they approached, the soft grass silencing any noise, the wind cutting across the moors helped too. The men surrounded the cottage, all pistols primed and cocked. One shot rang out as the captain fired a warning shot and the order to surrender. King slammed the lantern to the floor and his two men covered the door and window. King stood behind them brandishing his pistol. Turpin stood behind him weaponless. He launched himself at King reaching for the pistol and turning it into his fat belly. He fumbled for the trigger and pulled. King screamed out loud and hit the floor. Thinking that their leader was going to make a break for it, his two men started firing, only to be cut down by a volley of pistol fire. Turpin had dropped the pistol and stood with his hands raised in surrender. "Only one left to hang," someone shouted.

Chapter 10

Jonathan watched as the king walked the length of the spa unaided. "Very good, Sire, it is now time for you to return to London and you will soon be able to carry on with your duties and I can go home."

The king thanked Jonathan again and asked him if he was ready to go home. "No doubt, you are missing your family and of course, the lovely Lady Patricia."

"Yes, your majesty, you are correct, is it so obvious?"

The king looked at Jonathan. "There's something not quite right here, Doctor, why don't you open up to me?"

Jonathan turned away feeling ashamed. "Because, Sire, I'm of low birth, Lord Fairbanks does not recognise me as suitable for his niece's hand in marriage. It is important that Lady Patricia marries someone of high status who will be able to provide security for Lady Patricia and of course, their stately home 'Boughey Hall'."

The king nodded and stroked his chin. "Of course, I do understand these things, Jonathan, it is important for one to maintain a standard of living and even more so for titled people, the so-called aristocrats of our nation. They do not want to lose what they have gained and only want to maintain a standard they have risen to. It is only fair for them to protect their offspring and want the best for them. It is also my way of thinking but still, I do see true love when it blossoms. These so-called nobles have done something to earn their status. Many have earned their titles during military campaigns or some form of servitude to their reigning monarch or even contributed something to their country. I'm sure, Jonathan, if you had a daughter she would be rated as a prominent doctor's daughter and you would want the best for her. Would you want her to marry below her status, a stable hand for instance or a farm labourer?" Jonathan agreed with the king's summoning up of the situation, it was true but still unfair.

The king changed the subject. "Tomorrow before you depart for home, I want you to see me enter the grand hall on my legs like a King should do. There's to be a grand ceremony attended by all palace personnel. You will be there, Jonathan, to see my grand entry. My secretary will accompany you. After the ceremony, you will be free to slip away. I understand you declined the offer of my coach and have booked your seat on the northern coach. I want to express my sincere gratitude to you, Jonathan, and if ever you should decide, there will always be an appointment here for you as my personal physician but of course, you would have to live here at the palace."

Jonathan thanked the king and departed to his room where he started packing his belongings. If the ceremony finished by lunchtime, he would be in plenty of time for the two o'clock coach. The thought of seeing Lady Patricia occupied his mind.

Next morning, he had breakfast and prepared himself for the ceremony. The secretary arrived at ten thirty to see if Jonathan was ready. The palace was humming with courtiers and ministers and all sorts of high-status officials, all lined up around the grand hall to witness the king's entrance. The secretary pushed their way to the front, occupying a position very close to the throne, which unnerved Jonathan a bit. The ensemble stood there in silence waiting for the trumpets to herald the grand entry. The people gathered coughed and shuffled impatiently, suddenly the sound of trumpets echoed around the grand hall as the king in a full ceremonial dress made his grand entrance. Everyone bowed gracefully as the king stood unaided in front of the throne. He sat down and the hall filled with a tumultuous round of applause. The king waved and waited for the applause to fade away before addressing the members of his royal court.

"My lords, ladies and gentlemen, due to a riding accident I have been away from my duties as your king but now as you can see I am completely recovered. My recovery is due to a young doctor from the county of Staffordshire, who I was most fortunate to make his acquaintance. This young doctor whose name is Jonathan Godwin dedicated his untold skills and precious time to tending my injuries. Without his expertise and untold devotion, I would never have walked again. His skills go beyond the normal doctors' knowledge and even beyond my own medical staff. I have been very fortunate and this ceremony here today is not just to welcome your King back but to reward Doctor Jonathan Godwin for his skill and dedication given to his King. Please step forward Doctor Jonathan Godwin and accept this reward."

The secretary pushed Jonathan towards the king. A courtier had put a cushion on the floor in front of the throne. The king stood up and asked Jonathan to kneel on the cushion. Another courtier approached the king with a jewel-encrusted ceremonial sword. "Jonathan Godwin, it is an honour for me as your King to bestow upon you a knighthood for your dedicated service to your King." The king lowered the sword and touched Jonathan on each shoulder. "Arise, Sir Jonathan Godwin, Knight of the Realm."

Jonathan was shaking like a leaf. He looked up at the king as the ceremonial sword was taken away. The king reached out his hand to Jonathan. "Now, Jonathan, go and marry Lady Patricia." The room exploded with applause as the secretary accompanied and escorted Jonathan back to his room.

"Well, I never expected that," said Jonathan. The secretary shook his hand. "Well, Sir Jonathan, you deserved it, now as a nobleman, you are well qualified to marry your Lady and the king has dispatched letters to Lord Fairbanks recommending you for various duties, I'm sure you won't be disappointed."

Jonathan sat back on the coach, his mind still in a whirl. At every bump in the road, he expected to be suddenly awakened from his dream. At Northampton, he could hardly sleep and was glad to hear the cock crow heralding a new day. When he glimpsed the spires of Lichfield cathedral, he was wondering what to say to his mother and father. Could he just say "I'm now Sir Jonathan Godwin knight of the realm" or "How have you been all this time?"

The short journey from Lichfield to Rugeley took little time; the light hire carriage was soon pulling in at the surgery. Jonathan paid the driver and gathered his luggage. Edward greeted him first and then his mother and father met him at the door. A huge hug from both of them and he was sitting at the table with a glass of elderberry wine. Questions came from all directions. "How long are you here for and how is the king?"

Jonathan was overwhelmed. He waited for all the excitement to die down before standing up and addressing his parents.

"I have an announcement to make which I think will warrant something stronger than the elderberry wine." He unfurled the royal parchment the king had presented him with. Doctor John was first to take it in. "Good gracious mother, the king has given our son a knighthood." Mrs Godwin almost collapsed with excitement as she gazed at the royal parchment.

"Well, what a wonderful surprise and an honour for our son. I'll just get something stronger to put in these glasses. Edward come in, Jonathan has been knighted by the king."

When everybody had calmed down, Doctor John asked if Lady Patricia knew about it. "No, not yet, I was going to see her later and tell her the news." Doctor John stood up and looked at Mrs Godwin. "I think we had better tell him, my dear." Jonathan looked puzzled. "Tell me what, Father?"

"Jonathan, we have just heard the news about Lieutenant Samuel Hagleigh. He has been killed on a battlefield in France and his remains are being brought up here to Hagleigh Hall for burial in the family plot in the church in Rugeley. Preparations are underway and it takes place in two days on the arrival of a mounted escort from his regiment. Can I suggest we keep a low profile until a little later perhaps?" Jonathan looked flabbergasted. "I didn't know anything about that. All I knew was that he had joined the military." Doctor John said he and Mrs Godwin were attending the burial service and that the streets would be packed with onlookers. A gun carriage had been brought up to carry the casket to the church. Jonathan agreed a low profile would be required at such a drastic time. "I shall not attend the service myself, neither will Lady Patricia. We both have our reasons so I will ride over to Boughey Hall on the day and spend time with her. My knighthood will remain confidential until a more suitable time but I will pay her a visit late this afternoon to let her know I'm back."

Mrs Godwin filled the glasses and even Edward joined in with the congratulations. "I will now have to call you Sir Jonathan, Master Jonathan; that may take some getting used to."

Lady Patricia shielded her eyes against the sun as she saw the rider coming towards the house. With bated breath, she moved closer to the window. She recognised the gait of the horse and exploded with a cry of delight. Rushing towards the French doors, she threw them open and rushed to greet Jonathan. She was in his arms before his feet touched the ground. He bent down and kissed her passionately. "Please do that more often, Jonathan, you don't know how I long for your kisses and embrace." They walked around the gardens and Jonathan was aware that Lord Fairbanks had been watching them from the library window. "You have heard about Lord Samuel Hagleigh, have you, Jonathan? Father will be attending the funeral but I won't." Lady Patricia had put her arm through Jonathan's as they walked. "Neither will I," said Jonathan, "there was no love between us as you know"

"Well, Lady Hagleigh blames me for his joining the military, so no doubt she also blames me for the death, there's no love lost between us and Lord Samuel wasn't for me."

Jonathan squeezed her hands. "Don't blame yourself for anything like that, Patricia, he was a nasty man with evil intentions."

They walked around the gardens and then entered the house. Lord Fairbanks greeted Jonathan with a firm handshake. "Well done, Jonathan and we must congratulate you."

Patricia looked at her uncle. "What for, what has he done to deserve congratulations, he's only returned home to us, haven't you, Jonathan?"

Lord Fairbanks glanced at Jonathan. "You haven't told her yet?" he whispered.

Jonathan shook his head. "No sir, I wanted to keep it low profile until after Lieutenant Samuel's funeral."

Lord Fairbanks nodded. "So be it, I'll say no more but we will need to get together shortly to make plans."

Lady Patricia entered the room with a tray of drinks. "Let's celebrate Jonathan's return."

The town was preparing for the funeral. The streets were cleaned and swept and all obstacles removed. Shops had half closed, their blinds and even the school children had been allowed to line the streets. Flags were at half mast and local dignitaries were lined up to follow the procession through the town to the church. At eleven o'clock, the church bell began to peel. As the gun carriage carrying the coffin emerged onto the main road, the company of horse soldiers from his regiment formed up led by Captain Blaine. A solitary drummer led beating a slow beat. Family members in their horse carriages followed solemnly through the streets of the town which was lined by the towns people all bowing their heads in respect. At the church, the coffin was lifted by six soldiers and carried into the church for the hour-long service. It was a touching scene as many said afterwards, the man had died for his country.

Jonathan and Patricia sat quietly in the drawing room. "Uncle has something to talk to you about," said Patricia, "but he's being very secretive, he won't confide in me."

Jonathan looked at her. "And I have something to tell you which may come as a surprise." He told her how he had confided with the king in his affection for her and the king had asked why didn't he marry her. When he had told the king what the problem was, his majesty had fully understood but had indicated that a nobleman can be granted status by various means and that by helping the king could be one of them, and Jonathan was sure that's why he had been granted a knighthood. He had also written to Lord Fairbanks but Jonathan didn't know what it was about.

The funeral service went very well, with many tears being shed for Lieutenant Samuel Hagleigh; another hero for Rugeley to honour and remember. Lord Fairbanks mingled with the guests at Hagleigh Hall but was avoided by Lady Hagleigh, who bore a grudge against Lady Patricia, blaming her for her son's death. Doctor Godwin and Mrs Godwin paid their respects and left early. Lord Fairbanks was also ready to leave and was just leaving the hall as Doctor and Mrs Godwin were doing so. He walked over and spoke to them, commenting on the sad affair. He then asked them if they would like to accompany him to Boughey Hall for drinks. They accepted gracefully, indicating that Doctor Jonathan was already there, keeping Lady Patricia company.

Jonathan and Patricia sat in the gardens enjoying the early evening aroma given off by the assortment of flowers surrounding the lawns and borders. "Here's uncle now," said Patricia, "and he's got company, I wonder who he's brought home with him."

Jonathan shaded his eyes. "That's my mother and father's carriage following him." They stood up and made their way to the large front entrance. Lady Patricia greeted her uncle and then turned her attention on the other carriage. "What a pleasant surprise," she said greeting them, "welcome to Boughey Hall, it has been a long time since we had the pleasure."

Doctor John helped his wife from the carriage. "Yes, my lady, it has, your uncle has cordially invited us back for drinks and I promise you, my dear, no cards on this occasion."

Lord Fairbanks led them into the drawing room where the butler started serving drinks.

"I'm so glad we can all be together for this occasion," said Lord Fairbanks, "I must admit I was planning something like this as I have matters of importance to discuss with Sir Jonathan Godwin and I think it is only proper that you should all be here to witness what I have to say." Lord Fairbanks stood up and raised his glass. "First, I would say let us drink a toast to our honoured guest and wish him good luck for the future." The glasses were raised and the toast drank. "I know that his knighthood was to be kept a low profile for the moment but I think we all know about it and we deserve to pay him our sincere best wishes." Lady Patricia held Jonathan's hand. "He has only just confided in me," she said, "it has taken me completely by surprise,"

After all the congratulations had died down, Lord Fairbanks again took the floor. "I would also like to inform you of the letters from the king to me, discussing a position more suiting a Knight of the Realm. The king has informed me or rather reminded me that due to my age, I should be retiring from his service as tax assessor for the crown and has nominated Sir Jonathan Godwin MD as my successor. My retirement takes place one year from now and his majesty has suggested I take Sir Jonathan Godwin MD under my wing for that period so that he can become familiar with his new role but I have yet to ask him if it is his wish to accept the position." Lord Fairbanks looked at Jonathan. "You do not have to answer now, take time to think about it, Jonathan." The room was full of surprised looks and gasps; everyone had been taken completely off their guard, Jonathan more than anyone. Lady Patricia had two complete surprises, first Jonathan's knighthood and now her uncle's offer to take him as his assistant and future royal tax assessor to the king. Another round of drinks was poured whilst everybody talked amongst themselves. Doctor John explained what a wonderful opportunity it was for his son and Jonathan was taken aback by Lord Fairbanks offer, it was totally unexpected and he was at a loss for words. Lady Patricia squeezed Jonathan's hand. Mrs Godwin was also at a loss for words and marvelled at the wonderful opportunity being offered her son.

Lord Fairbanks spoke again, saying that the king did so want to reward Jonathan for getting him back on his feet again and it was a wonderful chance for Jonathan if he decided to accept the offer.

As Doctor John and Mrs Godwin made their departure, Lady Patricia and Jonathan accompanied them to their carriage. It had been a somewhat unusual visit and there was a lot to talk about. Jonathan said he would be following shortly but first, he wanted to talk to Lady Patricia a while longer. Lord Fairbanks said he would talk to Jonathan again in a few days. As they sat in the drawing room, Lady Patricia looked at Jonathan. "I thought you would have accepted uncle's offer straight away," she said, a slight frown appeared across her brow. Jonathan took her hand. "I wanted to ask you if you will be my wife first." She drew closer to him. "Yes, Jonathan, you know I will but only if uncle would allow it."

He smiled at her. "Only if he allows you to be my wife will I accept his offer, those are my terms."

It was two days before Jonathan returned to Boughey Hall, determined to confront Lord Fairbanks with his proposal. *It's now or never,* he thought to himself.

The butler escorted him into the library and said he would notify Lord Fairbanks. Minutes later, the master of Boughey Hall entered, bidding the doctor a very good morning. "I take it you have given some thought to the offer, Sir Jonathan, and that this will call for a celebration." The butler placed drinks on the table.

"I want to marry Lady Patricia," Jonathan said quietly to Lord Fairbanks. "Will you give permission and your blessings?"

Lord Fairbanks looked hard at Jonathan. "You know how I cherish my niece," he said, "and I must look after her and her interests. I have seen you together many times and I know how you both feel about each other but it has always been my wish for Lady Patricia to marry a nobleman of some status. Well, Jonathan, the king has given you that status and also if you take on my position of Royal Tax Collector and assessor to the Crown of England, you will have all the credentials that I am looking for. Are you ready to accept the king's appointment?"

Jonathan rose from the chair and walked over to where Lord Fairbanks was standing. "If it means Lady Patricia and I can be married, then yes I accept most heartily."

Lord Fairbanks stretched out his hand. "I welcome you into my family, Sir Jonathan but I do ask for you to allow just one more year to get you ready to take on my position and all that it offers you." Jonathan accepted. "Now go and find Lady Patricia and tell her the good news."

Jonathan could hardly contain himself as he walked through the house searching for Lady Patricia. She had just come in from the gardens. "We must get together to sort out our wedding plans, we have a year to wait but that will allow us to arrange everything." Lady Patricia clapped her hands. "Oh Jonathan, has uncle said we can, I'm so thrilled!" She planted a big kiss on his lips. "That will do for a start." She giggled.

Doctor John and Mrs Godwin were thrilled with the news and Mrs Godwin poured out drinks to celebrate the good news. "You will have to talk seriously now to Lord Fairbanks, he will be your employer from now on, Jonathan. I doubt if you will have much spare time for our practice, medical matters must be put on one side now you have a new future to look forward to, a much more rewarding one, I may say."

Jonathan and Patricia spent more time together now and Lord Fairbanks always welcomed him to Boughey Hall. "We shall be shortly doing the rounds for the first time this year, Jonathan, if you can spend some time with myself and my clerk we will go through the procedure required for assessing the new taxes and then we will visit the persons concerned and collect this year's donations from the nobles and others." Jonathan scanned through the ledgers the clerk placed before him indicating what had been declared by the tax pages and what percentage had been assessed for payment to the crown. It seemed a fair way each person's tax based on what he declared as income, and an assessment was made as to whether his taxes were increased or remained the same. This procedure occurred every four months so taxes were collected by Lord Fairbanks three times a year. The journey covering the Staffordshire and Moorlands area could take up to a month to complete, which meant time away from Boughey Hall every four months. The king paid Lord Fairbanks according to how much was collected. It was a good living he said to Jonathan. He also took Jonathan into his confidence in the running of the estate. Whilst money was coming into the estate from rentals of land and farming assets, that alone was only just enough to pay for the upkeep of Boughey Hall additional monies needed to be earned. Lady Patricia had a small inheritance but that would not last forever. Jonathan would need to earn himself and that is why Lord Fairbanks was eager for him to take on his duties as tax assessor and collector when he retired.

Over the next few months, Sir Jonathan managed to help out at the running of the infirmary as well as his duties at Boughey Hall. Lady Patricia would ask him to join her whenever he could to discuss wedding plans. It had already been decided that Boughey Hall was to be their residence. Lord Fairbanks would also occupy a part of the house and convert it into a modest dwelling for himself and a small staff. The reception would be held in the main hall at the house with additional staff brought in temporarily to handle the catering. It wasn't to be a lavish wedding; Lady Patricia didn't want that despite her uncle's offer to pay all expenses. She wanted it over and done with quickly so that she and Jonathan could get down to living as man and wife.

The time for collecting the taxes soon came around and Jonathan was handed the ledger with all the names listed. They would take the coach and head north to the nobles who lived furthest away and then work their way down country back to Boughey Hall. The clerk, Lord Fairbanks and Jonathan occupied the coach comfortable seat whilst the driver and three armed soldiers made themselves comfortable outside. Four horses pulled the coach as the load would increase with the monies collected.

They managed two stately homes the first day with overnight accommodation included. The third noble lived a few miles from the city of York, a pleasant lord of the manor who offered food and shelter and was eager to have a long chat with Lord Fairbanks once the taxes were settled. "Well, at least you won't have to worry about highwaymen," he chortled, pouring out the wine. "They hung the last one yesterday, a chap called Turpin, I believe"

Jonathan's blood froze as he heard the name. "What did you say his name was?" he asked casually.

"I think it was Dick Turpin, a member of some gang called the Essex Gang from down south."

Lord Fairbanks and his clerk said it was a good thing. "Where did they hang him?" asked Jonathan, again trying to sound casual.

"York, and on the gibbet of the moors. Left him hanging for the crows to peck at."

His lordship seemed to find it amusing. Jonathan was frustrated, he had to get to York fast to find out where Bess had been stabled. "How far is it to York from here, I have a friend who lives there, haven't seen him for years."

Lord Fairbanks and the clerk were more interested in playing cards than in the conversation Jonathan was having with his lordship. "It's an hour's ride from here, Jonathan, if you wanted to visit him I can lend you a good horse."

Jonathan didn't need to ask twice. "That's very kind of you sir, I will accept your offer and set off at once."

Within the hour, Jonathan was entering the city's outskirts and began trawling the boarding stables looking for Bess. He tried half a dozen, zigzagging the city streets. It was late evening when he came across a fettler shoeing a black horse. "That's a fine-looking horse, who does that belong to?" he asked.

The fettler looked up at Jonathan. "It doesn't belong to anyone now," he said, picking up the old shoe, "I'll be selling her now." Jonathan stroked the mare. "It used to belong to a highwayman but they hung him yesterday and left him hanging on the gibbet. There were four of them to start with but three got shot in a confrontation with the law enforcers."

Jonathan didn't want to appear too interested. "Oh yes, I heard about that, Dick Turpin or somebody like that wasn't it?"

The fettler put his tools away. "I'll be locking up for the night now sir, is there anything I can do for you?"

Jonathan reached inside his coat pocket and pulled out his bag of gold coins. "Yes, I am here on a mission of importance. I think you might be the right person for the job. Is there an undertaker around these parts?" The fettler looked up and smiled. "Yes sir, that's another part of my job, I make the coffins for the deceased and the city pays me for 'em."

Jonathan peered at him in the lamplight. "I want Dick Turpin taken down and buried out on the moor. Could you do that, my man?"

The fettlers beady eyes fell on the gold coins as Jonathan started to count them out. "Yes, sir, I certainly can do that, all part of my job, sir." Jonathan stopped counting at 20. "How much, sir, for you to give Dick Turpin a decent burial?"

The fettler looked around his premises. "I've got a coffin already made up that will do," he said rubbing his stubbly chin.

"I'll give you 30gold sovereigns to do the job but make sure you do a good job and bury Mr Turpin out on the moors near the highway, do you understand and keep quiet about it. Also put that shoe off the mare in the coffin."

The fettler looked at Jonathan. "Was he a friend of yours, sir?"

Jonathan shook his head. "No but he saved my life sometime ago, I owe him for that and how about the mare, how much for her?" The fettler's beady eyes watched as Jonathan started counting. "I'll give you another 20, that's 50 gold sovereigns for you to bury Mr Turpin out on the moor and for the mare, and I also want you to be discreet about it, do you understand?"

The fettler held out his grubby hand as Jonathan started counting. "Yes sir, I'll be very discreet about it. I'll do it first thing in the morning before it gets light, nobody will see me." Stroking the mare, Jonathan said he would be back at noon to collect her and to pay the other half of the money.

Feeling as though his mission had been accomplished, he found himself a small tavern with accommodation and retired for the night.

A bright sunny day greeted Jonathan as he rode into the fettler's yard. His cart was there so it was a fair assumption that the fettler had completed his mission. Bess was in her stall and had been groomed and saddled. "Job done, sir," said the fettler emerging from the shadows and the horse ready for the road. "Did anyone see you?" Jonathan asked.

"No sir, not a soul about at five o'clock in a morning. I take it you don't want anyone to know where he's buried?"

Jonathan shook his head. "I don't suppose anybody will care about him."

The fettler handed him the bridle. "Well, there's the shepherdess he was living with, I thought they were a bit close."

Doctor Jonathan led Bess out of the yard. "Well, only if she enquires, maybe just her."

The afternoon sun was waning as he rode up to the mansion. Lord Fairbanks viewed him from the drawing room and came out to meet him. "Sir Jonathan, you have acquired another horse, and a fine-looking mare she is." The lord of the manor offered to lay on an evening meal if they required it but Lord Fairbanks declined, insisting that they had better get started on their homeward journey. The coach was brought to the front of the house and loaded up. Sir Jonathan shook hands with his lordship and said he looked forward to his next visit.

It was late at night as the noise of the coach's wheels echoed on the gravelled driveway. The butler came out to meet them and all the luggage was unloaded. The coach carrying the taxes was locked in the coach house under armed guard.

"Everyone has retired for the night, my lord," said the butler.

"Yes and so will we," suggested Lord Fairbanks.

Jonathan woke to a slight tapping on the door and a smiling Lady Patricia entered the room. "Jonathan Godwin, why did you deny me your presence last night, I was looking forward to a passionate kiss from you." She jumped on the bed and smothered him with kisses.

"Patricia the servants will see or hear you, it isn't ladylike, is it, but I am enjoying it." It was difficult to ignore the passion Lady Patricia plied on him but Jonathan remained the perfect gentleman and fought off the urges.

"It won't be long, darling for our wedding; we can refrain from any temptations until then." Lady Patricia though disappointed left the bedroom.

Over breakfast, Lady Patricia talked of nothing else except the forthcoming wedding. Lord Fairbanks said that they would be busy over the next few days accounting for the taxes and the ledgers which had to be ready for when the coach from London would be picking them up. Jonathan assured Patricia that there would be plenty of time during the evening when they would get some time to themselves to discuss the wedding plans which was a long way off yet. "But Jonathan, my wedding dress will have to be made and that could take ages, I want the best designers from London to come and take measurements." Lord Fairbanks left the table and said he would be seeing Jonathan in the office shortly.

"Let's get these accounts done first and then I will give you my undivided attention," promised Jonathan.

Lord Fairbanks' clerk had everything laid out on the desk when they finally arrived and at once opened up the ledgers for the accounting. "Now, Sir Jonathan, everything has to be totalled up and checked against the cash collected. When that has been balanced up, then all contributions are totalled up and if that all balances up, then the distribution can begin. The king's money has to be set aside first and then other distributions have to be made. For instance, Lord Fairbanks' costs and now of course yours also and also my meagre wages. It all takes time, sir but must be done before the coach from London arrives." Lord Fairbanks tapped his finger on a thick ledger. "And also our own records which must tally with the king's. This is my last accounting, Jonathan, next time it will be up to you and my clerk here. I shall be most glad to hand over my duties to you and I shall just melt into the background and enjoy my retirement." He raised the glass of wine that had been provided. "Here's to you, Jonathan Godwin, the new Lord Fiscal to his majesty." Jonathan raised his glass.

"Will I be a Lord then?" he asked with a huge smile on his face.

"Yes, Sir Jonathan Godwin, Lord Fiscal to the King of England," said the clerk also raising his glass, "that, sir, is now your official title from now on."

Lady Patricia clapped her hands with joy when Jonathan announced his real title. "Oh! Jonathan Lord Fiscal, you are now a real nobleman, darling." Lady Patricia wanted to talk about the wedding and Jonathan listened to all the plans she had made. She, of course, wanted the finest dressmakers in the area brought in to start on her wedding dress. Jonathan said his mother would like to come and lend and hand and asked Patricia if it would be alright. "Of course Jonathan, I would love her to help me choose, ask her to come, please."

Jonathan broke the exciting news to his parents when he finally managed to get away from Lady Patricia. Mrs Godwin said it would be an honour and asked Doctor Godwin when they would be able to make time. Doctor Godwin said that in a couple of days he would take time off from the infirmary and they could visit Boughey Hall then.

Jonathan said he would pay a visit to the monastery to see Brother Thomas. He was greeted with surprise, the monk did not know of Doctor Jonathan's return from London. A glass of elderberry wine was handed to him and Thomas asked Jonathan to tell all. The doctor explained all that had happened and expressed his gratitude for all the information he had been given by Thomas. He also expressed how good the rubbing oil had been. Brother Thomas explained how the Chinese use herbs such as mint, clove, cinnamon and eucalyptus to make their medicines and Brother Thomas would always receive a fine supply of herbs every six months from China. He said he also experimented with herbs. Jonathan asked how he knew which was alright and which was poisonous. "I have my method of testing," said Thomas, "I take a herb and rub it on my arm, if it causes a rash I do not use it, if it doesn't, I rub it on my lips. If there is no reaction, I taste it. If it makes me sick, I discard it. Very simple, Jonathan." He poured another glass of wine. "But you see this elderberry is very good."

Jonathan handed back the skeleton. "The king was very impressed and has bestowed a knighthood on me for getting him walking. I think he should do the same for you, Thomas."

The monk smiled. "I shall get my rewards in due course," he said, pointing a finger to the sky, "it keeps me happy doing what I do, what more can I ask for."

Jonathan mentioned the Western Towers infirmary. "I think some of your remedies could be well used there, I shall mention this to my father. They get most of the medicines from the apothecary but he doesn't have everything. It was your medicines that helped the patients at the convent, Thomas, especially those smelly sticks, even the king found them refreshing."

Brother Thomas reached for a handful. "Some new ones for you, Doctor Jonathan. The Chinese use them for burning incense but I have adopted them for freshening the air and also herbal remedies."

Jonathan emptied his glass of Elderberry wine. "I also have been given a new role. I take over Lord Fairbanks position as Lord Fiscal to the king. I am now responsible for tax collecting and tax assessment for the north and south Staffordshire country, including the Staffordshire moorlands. I shall not have much time for my medical duties but I will assist where I can but for now, my wedding to Lady Patricia Fairbanks has priority over everything." Brother Thomas expressed his congratulations and best wishes and said he would always be at the monastery if Jonathan should want him.

Chapter 11

The dress designers and seamstresses spent two weeks at Boughey Hall. Lady Patricia sent the coach to pick them up from surrounding counties. They brought all the materials and catalogues they could collect and were given access to the drawing room as their workshop. Soon Boughey Hall became a hive of activity. Jonathan spent time shopping in various towns for his wedding clothes. Mrs Godwin was as excited as anyone and insisted that Doctor Godwin and she should spend a day buying new clothes for the occasion.

Boughey Hall was a buzz of excitement and as the days drew near, it grew more hectic. Lord Fairbanks had the carriage taken away and refurbished to a high standard. The hall itself would also be spruced up and the gardens attended to. The wedding date was set for September 25th. The church in the town had been booked. The ceremony would last at least an hour and then everyone would make their way to Boughey Hall where a grand reception was being laid on. Lady Patricia was taking care of the invitations on her side of the family and Mrs Godwin took care of their side, although there weren't many to worry about as their family was small compared to Lady Patricia's.

It had been decided that only friends and family living within a 30-mile radius would be invited. There were to be no overnight guests as Lady Patricia and Jonathan were spending their honeymoon at Boughey Hall and maybe, find somewhere to go for a holiday when all the excitement had died down. So every guest would be capable of departing for their own homes at midnight when the celebrations would end. It was estimated that at least 30 coaches would attend with their guests. It would lead to a long procession from the church after the service and the groom and stable hands would be responsible for the parking. Every little detail was discussed and the floral decorations had to be arranged.

Doctor John was kept busy at the Western Towers infirmary and Sir Jonathan would put in an appearance whenever he could. Doctor John was pleased with the way things were going. He discussed the possibility of an infirmary in the town for the local people but said it would take some doing and only if the traders and local businessmen would be prepared to donate or invest in such a project, and where was there a suitable building in the town; it was a dream to be pondered on.

At last, the day of the wedding arrived and pandemonium broke out as Boughey Hall became the centre of attraction. Coaches began to arrive in Rugeley and sort parking places around the church. Some streets were closed, simply to accommodate the wedding guests and the people of the town thronged the streets ready to see Lady Patricia arrive. Doctor John and Mrs Godwin arrived with Sir Jonathan and for the first time, he looked nervous. He was escorted to a private room to await the appointed time. His best man stayed with him and was secretly given a glass of wine by the butler. A bell rang from the bell tower to announce the time had come to make the journey into town and to the church. One last sup of wine and they were in the coach waiting for them.

It was a fine day with lots of sunshine which encouraged the town's people to throng the streets. Shouts of congratulations echoed around the church as Jonathan and his best man walked up the path and through the church doors. Some of the guests were already seated but many still waited outside for the arrival of the bride. As the coach carrying Lady Patricia drew near the crowd became more excited. They obviously had special feelings for her.

The ceremony lasted an hour. Jonathan was glad when finally the ring was placed on Patricia's finger, sealing their undying love. It was another hour before the column of carriages arrived at Boughey Hall to be met by the maids and servants. The guests made for the great Hall where they were seated in order of importance. Lord Fairbanks sat at the head of the table next to the bride and groom. Speeches were made and soon the reception got underway. Jonathan leaned over and whispered to Patricia, "You are the most beautiful woman in the world, I am so lucky." Glasses were filled and raised and toasts made. Jonathan had recited his speech over and over again but when the time came to give it, he became tongue-tied and got some things mixed up. His best man helped out by prompting him. Nevertheless, it was received very well and raised great applause. The guests made their way to the drawing room and served drinks whilst the great hall was cleared for the dancing and musical entertainment. Jonathan danced with his bride but was also seconded by many of the female guests and Lady Patricia was also the most popular partner by many male guests. The evening was a happy occasion and dragged on until the bell was rung indicating the end of the evening. Slowly, the guests departed, many lingering to offer their congratulations. Lord Fairbanks had retired early. Doctor John and Mrs Godwin were the last to depart. Mrs Godwin hugged Patricia and gave Jonathan a huge hug. Doctor John gave his blessings and left holding onto his wife. The servants and the butler had tidied up a bit but was told by Jonathan to lock up and retire. Tomorrow had been granted a day off for all staff except for a skeleton staff.

They climbed the stairs to their private quarters and retired for the night enjoying the pleasures they had so waited for. The following morning, Jonathan woke up early just as daybreak was breaking. Patricia lay fast asleep. He gazed at here beautiful face. Getting dressed, he went outside and walked towards the meadow. Bess came up to him and he stroked her head. "She's a lovely mare," said Lord Fairbanks approaching Jonathan. "Yes, she is," said Jonathan, surprised at the sound of Lord Fairbanks. "You are up early." Patricia's uncle said that he liked the fresh air in the morning. "Let's walk around the gardens, shall we? I wanted a chance to have a little chat with you, Jonathan. I just want to say how pleased things have turned out for you and Patricia. I am very glad you are established. I can now blend into the background. I shall, of course, enjoy a game of cards with visiting friends and of course, your father. I shall also find myself a hobby and maybe travel a bit but most of all I am delighted that you have taken on my duties. I want to shake your hand, Jonathan, or should I call you, Sir Jonathan Godwin MD Lord Fiscal to the King of England, and now I hand over another title, you are now Master of Boughey Hall."

Part II

Chapter 12

Doctor John seemed very excited. Mrs Godwin asked him why he was in such a good mood. At the wedding reception, he had been talking to Sir Albert Thoroughgood, the entrepreneur who had a wool spinning factor in the town. He had this large building on Queen Street which he had adapted to a profitable business but now was not big enough for expansion. He wanted to incorporate it into a weaving and dying plant. Sir Albert was a wealthy man and lived in a very large house just out of town. His wife, Lady Laura Anne and four children, Albert Jnr, Florence, Hilda and Harry, all lived at home but did not get involved with the spinning business. Sir Albert was now looking for larger premises to expand his business but had so far found nothing suitable. An American colleague had suggested Sir Albert should move to America, an up and coming country with great prospects. He planned a short visit and he and Lady Laura would search for something suitable. The children however did not like the idea; they had heard about the wild Indians and decided they wanted to stay in England despite the wild uprising from Scotland and Wales. Doctor John had asked Sir Albert what was going to be done with the building in Heron Street. Sir Alfred said it could be sold off or leased out, the income of which would take care of the family left behind. Doctor John had asked him if it was possible for the building to be turned into an infirmary for the people of Rugeley. Sir Alfred said it was possible if the price was right. Doctor John had immediately consulted the town's governors and had also approached the town's traders who showed interest.

Sir Alfred said if everything went favourably, he would offer the spinners a chance to immigrate to America if they wanted to and help build up his new venture. Some did but some were reluctant and decided to stay in England.

Sir James Godfrey had made enquiries as to whether his troops were allowed back into the town now for recreational purposes, on the promise that senior military personnel would oversee their behaviour and promised that no trouble would arise.

This, of course, boosted the town's income and once again the flow of farm produce began.

Sir James had trained almost a thousand men on the ranges but the king had insisted on more. He wanted the finest marksmen ready for the French or the Welsh or the Scots to attack England. Already skirmishes in France had started.

Sir Jonathan visited his mother and father, taking Lady Patricia with him. A great fuss was made of her and Mrs Godwin was ecstatic when Patricia addressed her as a mother.

Doctor John told Jonathan of his plans for an infirmary in the town and Jonathan said it was a good thing and would help all he could. "I must leave you now," said Doctor John, "I have an important appointment with Lord Fairbanks; I think a game of cards has been arranged."

A few days later, Doctor John approached some of the local traders in the town, telling them of his plan and was met favourably with great interest. Questions were asked about what donations would be required but of course, as he explained, it was early days yet and the town governors had to be approached regarding permission to carry out the plans. The farmers and other traders were also approached and showed great interest providing the price wasn't beyond their means. Doctor John also called on Sir Albert Thoroughgood and asked if he had made up his mind about going to America. Sir Albert informed him that passage to America had been arranged for himself and Lady Laura, who were going for a short visit and to look around. He said Doctor John would be the first to know of their decision on their return. He also said that the family had shown great interest in the doctor's plans for an infirmary. Florence had always been interested in nursing and the boys were already in the construction business, so perhaps Doctor John could make use of them.

Lady Patricia made it clear that Mrs Godwin would be welcome to visit Boughey Hall at any time and hoped it would be soon.

The next few months passed by quickly. The town seemed to prosper and everyone seemed happy. Of course, there was always talk of war with France but with the town being quite distant away from the southern coast, nobody paid too much attention to it, although it was always a topic in the town and wherever groups of people met.

Sir Albert and Lady Laura Anne had returned from America full of enthusiasm. Doctor John had approached the governors of the town and had received their permission to proceed, providing Sir Albert had made up his mind. In fact, he had and discussed with Doctor John, rental terms which were to be paid to his children for their upkeep of the family residence. Now the spinning factory had been closed down and all the machinery was being shipped to America. Sir Albert had purchased a rundown cotton plantation with lots of room to develop. He planned to get his factory up and running as soon as possible. The mansion was being refurbished and his plans to cash in another cotton spinning and dying process along with the wool spinning was meeting with great enthusiasm. When the building in Heron Street had been cleared out, he invited the town's traders to an informal meeting there with Albert Thoroughgood Jnr and family also in attendance. Albert explained the possibility of alterations to the building with private rooms on the second floor and also an open ward for less serious complaints. The ground floor would contain a reception area, a private consultation room, a dispensary and some private rooms for nursing staff and of course for the matron, who happened to be Florence Thoroughgood. The meeting went favourably and Doctor John said he would hold another meeting soon to discuss donations before anything could get started. The Thoroughgood brothers would work out approximate costs and submit them to the doctor.

Within a month, everything had fallen into place. Doctor John was very happy with the way things had worked out. The planning had gone through, the governors had the approval of the idea and the Thoroughgood brothers were busy with the alterations. A second meeting with the traders and shopkeepers had gone favourably and a contract with the apothecary to supply medicines was in progress. Sir Albert and Lady Thoroughgood had departed for America to start their business so everything was going well.

Lord Fairbanks dealt the cards, he looked at his clerk and then at Doctor Godwin, a smile crossed his lips, indicating he had dealt himself a good hand. The stakes weren't too high, so the other two allowed Lord Fairbanks a little leeway, keeping him on a winning streak. "You should allow yourself an early retirement," he said to Doctor John, "I'm all for it." Doctor John gave a smile. "Too busy with healing the sick?" he murmured. "By the way, how's your gout?" Lord Fairbanks played his winning card. "It's fine now, I've gone over to the fruity wine your son introduced me to."

Sir Jonathan was in the meadow with the horses. Edward was with him. "Are you going to ride Black Bess?" he enquired.

"Yes Edward, will you take her to the stables and saddle her up please, it's about time she went for a run." He mounted Bess and steered her around the stable, he felt comfortable with her and she responded well to his gentleness, he felt sure that Dick Turpin would have approved.

Lord Fairbanks looked up from his cards and gazed out of the window as Jonathan rode by. "Our boy has settled in well," he said to Doctor John.

Jonathan took Bess out on the road and decided to visit the farms on the estate. He hadn't really explored all that now came under his charge. The farms had been doing well and produced milk, cheese, meat and other products for the town. Jonathan wondered if the infirmaries would benefit from buying directly from the estate instead of dealing with unscrupulous outside traders. On one of the farms, he also noticed a stable block with only a couple of horses in it. If that was extended it could accommodate more horses and furthermore a large parcel of land on the farm could be developed as a sort of training area. His mind was full of ideas as he made his rounds.

Lady Patricia greeted him on his return. "You haven't eaten your breakfast, Jonathan, so I'll arrange an early lunch. I think your father is about to depart minus a few sovereigns."

Jonathan gave her a quick kiss. "I just want a quick word with father, I won't be long."

Doctor John had just mounted his horse. "Morning, Jonathan, did you enjoy your ride, she's a good-looking mare." Jonathan asked his father to spare him five minutes. He mentioned that the farms were doing well and producing plenty of milk and cheese and other products. He asked Doctor John if he thought the infirmaries would benefit from cheaper products. "I would imagine they would," said the doctor. "I'll have a word with Hilda Thoroughgood, she's in charge of such things, maybe she can pay you a visit and see what can be arranged." Jonathan bade farewell to his father and joined Patricia for lunch.

Lord Fairbanks had received letters from the king expressing how pleased he was with the tax collection and had asked how Sir Jonathan had taken to it. There was also a small parcel included with strict instructions to be passed on to Sir Jonathan and Lady Patricia. Lord Fairbanks asked them to join him in his quarters. Full of curiosity, they paid him a visit after lunch. He handed Jonathan a letter from the king addressed to Sir Jonathan Godwin MD Lord Fiscal to his majesty the king and then handed over the parcel. Lady Patricia took the liberty of opening whilst Jonathan read his letter. She was very excited as she opened the box. A most beautiful diamond crusted bracelet revealed itself and a beautiful gold ring for a gentleman bearing the royal crest.

There was also a short letter in the king's own handwriting congratulating them on their marriage and wishing them all the best. Jonathan's letter was full of praises for his outstanding performance as Lord Fiscal. He apologised for not being able to visit them as the trouble in France needed his constant attention. He also mentioned he was walking and riding very well.

Mrs Godwin had been putting in a lot of time at the Western Towers infirmary and was now showing signs of exhaustion. Doctor John had noticed and was concerned. He took his wife to one side and spoke to her about taking time off. The nursing staff were now fully trained and under the watchful eyes of a charge nurse were quite capable of looking after things. She agreed she needed a rest. Doctor John spoke to his son and said he was concerned. Jonathan agreed and suggested his mother should come and stay at Boughey Hall under the watchful eye of himself and Patricia. With the doctor spending most of the time with the practice and the infirmary, Mrs Godwin would be on her own all day at home. Doctor John agreed it would be better if Jonathan and Patricia didn't mind. Patricia jumped at the idea and the maids prepared one of the rooms for Jonathan's mother. Doctor John became a regular visitor to see his wife which of course delighted his lordship, who always had a deck of cards ready.

After two weeks of complete rest, Mrs Godwin seemed to improve a little but Jonathan was still concerned about her. She had lost the sparkle in her eyes and got tired if you stayed too long at her bedside. He decided he was going to give his mother a full medical examination despite her objections. He consulted his father who agreed to assist him.

Mrs Godwin argued that there was nothing wrong with her but Doctor John insisted that a full medical would not go a miss. Lady Patricia accompanied him to the bedroom. First, he checked her eyes and gradually worked his way down, much to Mrs Godwin's objections. However, listening to her heart caused the doctor to frown. He carried on with the examination. When Jonathan came into the room, Doctor John took him to one side and spoke to him in a low voice much to the annoyance of Mrs Godwin. Jonathan walked over to her bedside. "Don't get upset, Mother, we are only giving you a check up. Now calm down, I want to listen to your heart."

Jonathan did the examination, gave her a quick peck on the cheek and walked back over to where his father was standing. "Yes, there is something there," he said. They both walked over to Mrs Godwin who was being comforted by Lady Patricia. "We are going to put you on some medication, Mother," said Jonathan, "you have a slight irregularity in your heart, you must rest a while longer and see if the medication helps you."

Mrs Godwin looked at her husband. "What is Jonathan talking about?" she asked.

"Your heartbeat is a bit irregular, my dear, that's probably why you have been getting tired. You must rest now and not get upset or excited about anything, we are going to keep an eye on you."

Lady Patricia put her arms around Mrs Godwin. "That's lovely, now you are going to stay with us a while longer Mother."

Doctor John and Jonathan retreated downstairs where they could talk freely. "What do you think, Father?" asked

Jonathan. "Her heartbeat is irregular, sometimes too fast and sometimes too slow. Her heart is working hard, something is wrong. Let's try her on some medication and see if we can get it functioning right."

A week passed by, Doctor John sat on a chair next to his wife's bed. "How are you feeling now, my dear, is the medicine helping you?" He looked at her and listened to her heartbeat.

"I feel a little better but I've got a slight pain in my chest, is that the medication or what?"

Doctor John listened to her heartbeat. "It's still a bit irregular," he said, "maybe we need to increase the dosage a bit."

Jonathan was waiting at the bottom of the stairs for his father; he noticed the look of concern on his face. "She's not responding, is she?" he said.

Doctor John shook his head. "I'm concerned there may be a blockage in one of the arteries feeding her heart. The medication doesn't seem to be helping much, it's only a painkiller, after all, I'll go to the apothecary and see what else he's got."

Jonathan said he was going to the monastery to see his friend, Brother Thomas. He was greeted with a big smile as Thomas looked up from his herb garden. "Let's have a drink of my new dandelion wine," he suggested.

Jonathan sat down and tasted the wine. "Very nice," he said, "but Thomas, I want something else. My mother is ill, it's her heart." He related the symptoms to Thomas who reached for his famous book of medicines. After scanning through the pages and listening to Jonathan, he got up and reached for a small bottle on the shelf. "In China and most of the Asian countries, they use this medicine to clean the arterial system. Try this, one spoonful of the powder in a glass of warm water, three times a day and limit the food intake for two days while she is taking the medication. I think you will find this will help your mother, and also limit the intake of fatty foods which cause the arteries to get furred up." Jonathan thanked his friend and promised to collect more glassware from the glassworks.

Doctor John looked at the white powder and sniffed it, and he put a small sample on his tongue. "We can try, Jonathan, I know Brother Thomas is a very good herbalist and you have much faith in him."

For two days, the doctors kept a watchful eye on Mrs Godwin and Patricia sat with her for long periods at a time. On the third day, Jonathan entered the room, his mother was asleep. He looked down at her; she had a bit more colour in her cheeks and seemed to be breathing a lot easier. He decided to keep her on the medication Brother Thomas had given him for another two days but increased her food intake a bit more each day. Doctor John had also noticed the difference and said how good the medication had been and maybe consider getting some for the infirmaries.

With the Queen Street infirmary completed, Doctor John had his work cut out organising everything and had missed his wife's help. Florence Thoroughgood was very efficient as matron and kept everyone on their toes. Mrs Godwin had got on well with Florence and had worked well together. The newly trained nursing staff under Mrs Godwin's experienced hand had performed very well. Some of the spinners who had not gone with Sir Albert to America had welcomed the opportunity to retrain as nursing staff and Hilda

Thoroughgood saw to it that the cleanliness of the infirmary was absolute. Doctor John had asked her about the farm produce being purchased directly instead of being bought through various agents. "It was a good idea, let's try it for six months and see," she said.

The first patients soon started attending the infirmary. Doctor John held surgeries and admitted certain patients who needed special care. Jonathan would help when he could but it was obvious more doctors were needed. Jonathan said he would ask around. The surgery at Brier Cottage would now have to close down due to the pressure of having two infirmaries to look after. Jonathan took on some of the patients in the outlying areas but could only take on so much. He now had his own duties as Lord Fiscal as well as managing the Boughey Hall estate.

Mrs Godwin was responding well and Lady Patricia suggested she should now be allowed out of bed and should be free to roam the estate under her watchful eye. Doctor John agreed and soon they were walking around the gardens together and even calling in on Lord Fairbanks who was always glad of the company, even to the point of suggesting Mrs Godwin joins the card school but unknown to him, Mrs Godwin had been an ardent card player for years at her ladies circle of friends. Lord Fairbanks was soon aware of this when Mrs Godwin started walking away with the winnings.

It was about time for Jonathan to make his first round as Lord Fiscal on his own with only the clerk to accompany him. Of course, there would be an armed guard supplied by Sir James Godfrey who was still active out on Cank Thorn at the ranges. Lord Fairbanks had already briefed him in advance so Sir Jonathan Godwin MD set about planning his journey, which would take him away from the estate for a month. The clerk told Jonathan that they would do the rounds much quicker as Lord Fairbanks would spend a lot of time on wasteful gossip with the nobles, being sociable so to speak.

Jonathan suggested they make for the furthest call first, then work their way back through the country and if possible, avoid staying overnight at each stately home. Perhaps every other one would suffice suggested the clerk and if they could persuade all taxpayers that their accounts should be ready by the 30th of every quarter, maybe a lot of time would be saved.

Mrs Godwin was now fully recovered from her illness and was ready to go back to her duties at the infirmary. She would spend a few days at each one according to demand but watched over carefully by Doctor John. The Queen Street infirmary started to fill up quite soon after its opening day. A lot of injuries were sustained by the farm labourers and also children were prone to falling and breaking arms and legs. The traders and shop keepers expressed their appreciation and often donations of goods from the shops mysteriously would be left in the reception area.

Doctor John received a message from Lady Isabella and promptly went to see her. She had become depressed again and was feeling a bit lonely despite having her own staff around her. When Lady Patricia heard about it, she ordered the coachman to have the coach ready at the front door. She went to her uncle's quarters and asked him if he would accompany her on a visit to Western Towers. He said he would welcome a day out and they were soon on their way. Lady Isabella was very much surprised when her maid told her she had visitors. Lord Fairbanks greeted her enthusiastically. "It's been a long time Isabella since we last met, I do apologise but now that I have recently retired my visits can be more frequent."

Lady Isabella greeted them happily and expressed her pleasure. "It has been a long time indeed, you scoundrel, I remember the times when you came regularly for a game of cards with my husband, we had such fun, didn't we, and how is your beautiful niece, Patricia. My how beautiful she is, marriage suits you, my dear." Lady Patricia embraced Lady Isabella.

"It has been a few years since we last visited and we must say how sorry we are." They retired to the drawing room where drinks were served.

"Ah, yes, my dear, the good old days," said Lord Fairbanks, "you were good with the cards, Isabella, we must try it again, what say you?" Lady Patricia noticed a sparkle in Lady Isabella's eyes. Yes, she thought, get them together again; it would be good for both of them. They spent time walking around the garden admiring the fauna and a short walk along the river.

"Ah, here you all are," called out Doctor John from the French windows, "what a lovely day you have chosen to visit Lady Isabella."

Lady Patricia joined Doctor John. "I had forgotten what good friends they were, here's the solution to the problem of her loneliness, regular visits and a game of cards. That should stimulate both of them."

Doctor John smiled. "You may be right there, Patricia."

Sir Jonathan Godwin MD Lord Fiscal to the crown met the nobles and other taxpayers and got on well with them all, despite some objections when the taxes were increased but as Jonathan said the taxes were adjusted according to income, some paid more and some paid less. Deep in his heart, he felt as if some of them didn't declare honestly and falsified their receipts but provided some income was being provided for the crown showing a steady increase he turned a blind eye.

The rounds were completed in three weeks. As the clerk had said, Lord Fairbanks would extend his stay if a game of cards and a glass of wine was available.

Lady Patricia saw the coach coming along the driveway and waited at the door to greet Jonathan. The butler ordered the luggage to be unloaded and then the coach has laden with the tax collections taken to the coach house and kept under guard until the London coach came. "Oh Jonathan, I have missed you," she said locking her arms around him. They kissed and he whispered, "And I you." They walked arm in arm through the house and made their way upstairs. In the bedroom, Patricia again embraced her husband. "Jonathan, I want a baby," she said quietly in his ear. Jonathan squeezed her and planted a passionate kiss on her lips. "So do I," he whispered.

The London coach arrived two days later with their mounted escort and the taxes were handed over and signed for. Jonathan's armed escort climbed onto the coach and was dropped off at the ranges. Jonathan had slipped them a couple of sovereigns each as a thank you.

Mrs Godwin was happy to be back at work and got on well with Florence Thoroughgood, although a little bit stricter with the nursing staff but carried out her duties as matron perfectly. On the days she was at Western Tower, if it coincided with a visit from Lord Fairbanks and his clerk for an arranged game of cards, she was requested by Lord Fairbanks, if he saw her, to join them at the card table, much to Lady Isabella's delight. Everything was running smoothly. With the surgery at Briar Cottage now closed down, Edward asked the doctor if his services would still be required. Doctor John straight away assured Edward that he was still under full employment looking after the horses and general maintenance of the place with the occasional job of running Mrs Godwin about in the pony and trap. She, of course, spent her nights at home with Doctor John and would welcome being driven to work and collected again by Edward, who also found himself running errands for the infirmaries.

Lady Patricia suggested to Jonathan that he should examine her as she thought she might be pregnant. Much to her husband's examination and enthusiasm, she was. "Oh Patricia, I can hardly wait for our child to be born," he whispered as they lay in bed, "but I want you to take it easy from now on, a lot of things can go wrong during pregnancy, I have had to cope with a lot of emergencies and sadness during my years as a doctor." Patricia promised to relax more.

"Can we tell anyone yet?" she asked. Jonathan suggested she wait a month before they break the news to anybody.

It was a month later that Doctor John awoke to someone banging on the door at Briar Cottage. Edward notified the doctor that he was required at Western Towers. "It was thought that Lady Isabella had had a severe stroke. Mrs Godwin asked Edward to get the trap ready and she would follow Doctor John who had already dressed and was saddling his horse he told the messenger to ride to Boughey Hall and ask Sir Jonathan to join him at Western Towers as soon as possible. The night air was cold so Mrs Godwin wrapped up warm. Edward was driving the horse and trap as it was so late at night.

Lady Isabella was in bed in her own living quarters. When Doctor John arrived, he examined her and gave her some medication to relax her. Jonathan arrived shortly after, Mrs Godwin followed almost immediately. Jonathan confirmed his father's diagnosis. Lady Isabella had had a stroke. Lord Fairbanks and Patricia arrived quite soon; they had come by a coach driven by their groom. "How is she?" enquired Patricia. Mrs Godwin was sitting at her bedside talking softly to her whilst Doctor John and Jonathan did further tests. They stood to one side while Patricia spoke comforting words to her. The doctors were debating whether to have her moved into the infirmary or let her stay in her own quarters. Mrs Godwin suggested that Lady Isabella should be taken to a guest room in the infirmary where she would be looked after by nurses 24 hours a day. "Let her benefit by what she has gracefully donated," she whispered to the doctors, "we owe her that much."

Jonathan asked his father what he had given Lady Isabella in the way of medicine. "It's just a painkiller, a relaxative for the moment."

"What about trying her on the same medication we gave Mother to clear her arteries, do you think it may work as a clot-buster?"

Doctor John thought for a moment, the Chinese white powder had proved a success with Mrs Godwin. "It might be worth a try but we haven't got any yet, have we?"

Jonathan looked at his father. "No, not yet but I know someone who has." He left the room and rode off into the night. Patricia asked where Jonathan had gone. "To the monastery I think," said Doctor John.

Jonathan had to ring the bell several times before one of the monks came to the door. "I wish to see Brother Thomas at once. It is a matter of life or death." The monk let him in and said he would go and wake Brother Thomas. Yawning and bleary-eyed Thomas appeared. "Sir Jonathan, what brings you here at such an hour?" Jonathan explained what had happened and asked Thomas for some of the medicine. Thomas led him into his workshop and gave him a glass jar of the white powder. "I would suggest a small dose at first and watch for any reaction, it doesn't suit everyone but it is good as you found out with your mother."

Jonathan rode through the night at a fast pace. There was a full moon and the way was well lit. Lady Isabella had been moved into the infirmary and was lying comfortable and surrounded by her friends. Jonathan gave the medicine to his father. "Try a small dose first. Thomas said and watch out for any kind of reaction."

During the next two days, the white powder was given to Lady Isabella. At first, there was no reaction but on the third day, she came around and began to try and ask what had happened. Mrs Godwin was with her and comforted her. She explained in simple terms that Isabella had had a slight stroke which happens now and again to older people but she was not to worry as she was in good hands and would soon begin to feel better.

Doctor John and Jonathan paid her a visit and were pleased with the result. "You must ask Brother Thomas to supply the infirmaries with his magic powder," said Doctor John as he examined Lady Isabella. "That's twice it has worked wonders."

Lady Patricia was waiting for Jonathan to arrive home. She looked particularly happy. She embraced him and led him upstairs to the bedroom where she asked him to examine her. "I think I maybe pregnant," she blurted out."

Jonathan at once examined her "I think you may be right, how long it has been since your period?"

Patricia hugged him. "I'm over due by almost three weeks and getting bouts of nausea."

Jonathan said he was very pleased. "But keep it a secret a little bit longer until we are sure, meanwhile, take things easy and no heavy lifting." Jonathan planted a kiss on her lips. "I do hope you are, my dear."

"How is Lady Isabella?" asked Patricia. Jonathan said she seemed to be responding to treatment but it was early days yet.

Hilda and Florence Thoroughgood sat in the matron's office reading their father's letter. "He seems to be doing alright and mother's enjoying the climate. The wool spinning is underway and the cotton process has begun. Father has now got people advising him on the dyeing process. They sound very happy, we must show Albert and Harry father's letter."

Hilda said that the produce from the local farmers was saving them quite a lot of money and would continue to favour them, much to the disappointment of the previous suppliers. Matron commented on how well the infirmary was doing. "I wonder if we will ever see Mother and Father again, I hear America is dangerously populated with wild savages, I'm glad I'm not there," said Hilda.

"I think you are talking about the wild west part of America, where Mother and Father are has been tamed so I believe," said Florence, "anyway, I'm not going out there to find out."

Lady Patricia lay down on the bed; it was another day of feeling unwell. Mrs Godwin stood looking through the window as the groom was giving Bess a brush down. "I've seen that horse before but I don't know where," she muttered to herself. She sat on a chair beside Patricia. "You are pregnant, aren't you, my dear?" she said with a cheerful note in her voice. "You can't fool an old ex midwife like me. I know all the symptoms, it's about time you let us all into your secret." She gave a low laugh. "I'm going to be a grandmother, aren't I?"

Lady Patricia let her in on their secret. "Jonathan and I was waiting to make sure, I think we are certain now so our secret can be passed on."

Doctor John received a message from Lord Hagleigh requesting a visit. He made the call after checking in at the infirmary in Queen Street. Lord Hagleigh looked aged since Doctor John had seen him last, no doubt the loss of his son Samuel had been a great loss to him and was taking its toll. "No doctor, it's not me, it's my young son, Thomas. He took a fall at the gravel pits and gashed his leg which has now become inflamed and given him a nasty rash. He's up in his room if you wouldn't mind taking a look at him." Lord Hagleigh rang his bell and had a servant take the doctor up the stairs. Thomas was lying on his bed, Doctor John greeted him cordially and asked Thomas to show him his injury. "I didn't think much of it at the time," said Thomas, "but now it's very painful and inflamed."

Doctor John examined the wound. "Well, Lord Thomas, it appears to be a severe case of gravel rash which has become infected and if not treated, could turn to gangrene. I would suggest you come to the Western Towers infirmary and we can start treating you at once."

Lord Thomas looked at the doctor. "I hope you will forgive my family's attitude towards you, Doctor. They were completely out of order with their insinuations regarding Lady Patricia. I bear no malice or grudges towards you. Please count on me as a friend."

Doctor John shook the outstretched hand. "I'll tell your father to have you brought into the infirmary as soon as possible and I will go and make arrangements for your private room."

Lord Hagleigh said he would have his son taken to the infirmary and said how grateful he was to Doctor John for his quick response. He held out his hand and they shook.

Mrs Godwin began noticing Patricia was getting bigger but was trying to hide the bump with various clothing. "Nothing too tight," she said, "and stop trying to hide it, show it off and be proud." Jonathan spent as much time as he could on the estate, he didn't want to be too far away from Patricia but the next tax collection round was fast approaching. He didn't want to leave Patricia in her delicate condition and mentioned it to his mother who straight away volunteered to stay at Boughey Hall and take care of her daughter-in-law whilst Jonathan attended his duties. Doctor John agreed it was the best thing to do and he would be a regular visitor to check up on Lady Patricia.

Lord Fairbanks waved them off when the time came for them to depart on the king's business. Accompanied by an armed guard, they took the same route as before, heading up country to the first call. They were greeted favourably by all the nobles and country gentlemen and even the farmers were in a friendly mood having been treated fairly by the Lord Fiscal to his majesty.

The clerk said that since Jonathan had taken over the duties attitudes had improved a great deal. He had a better way of handling things. Lord Fairbanks had a harsh attitude to some of the patrons, especially on the Staffordshire Moorlands where the farming was harsher than South Staffordshire. Jonathan treated them fairly and was treated respectfully. The royal tax collectors went home fairly confident that they had dealt everyone equally, taking only what could be afforded but still they were satisfied with the king's taxes and headed home after three weeks. They were happily received on their return to Boughey Hall and Jonathan left the coach and ran inside the house to see Patricia. He was surprised to see how well she looked and noticed the waistline increasing. Mrs Godwin said now she could make an appearance at the infirmaries, they were busy and needed her help.

The coach was locked up and guarded and Jonathan helped the clerk with the ledgers, securing them in the clerk's apartment before hurrying back to Patricia. Patricia said she had noticed the extra weight she was carrying and said it was probably a buxom lad she was carrying. She led Jonathan into the room they had chosen for the nursery and it had already been stripped bare ready for decorating. She also said that her uncle had made a few visits to Lady Isabella and had struck up quite a friendship with her and now that she was recovering from her stroke, visited quite often for a game of cards. "I'm glad to hear it," said Jonathan, "it's the company for them both."

When the London coach arrived and the taxes were taken away, Jonathan breathed a sigh of relief. He didn't like keeping so much money on the property, without armed guards, it put everyone at risk from robbers. Lord Fairbanks said that the taxes were needed to fund the war that was building up in Havana besides keeping Napoleon at bay.

One evening, Lord Fairbanks failed to return home from a visit to Lady Isabella. Jonathan saddled his horse and he and a groom rode off to find out what had happened to his lordship. On reaching Western Towers, they made their way to Lady Isabella's living quarters, only to find half a dozen people around the card table making a right raucous. Wine was being consumed and money was being gambled. When Jonathan entered the room Lord Fairbanks was not to be seen. A well-lubricated Lady Isabella tried to stand up and address Jonathan. Lord Fairbanks it seemed had consumed quite a lot of wine that evening and had passed out under the influence. The other members of the card game, well known to Jonathan, had put Lord Fairbanks to bed to sleep it off. Jonathan bid the party good night and left. Lord Fairbanks arrived somewhere around lunchtime the next day.

Lady Patricia was now putting on weight and was showing signs of tiredness. Jonathan told her now was the time to hand over the household duties to the staff and to relax more. It was now the seventh month and Patricia needed to rest more often. Jonathan allowed her to walk in or around the garden but no more and always accompanied by her maid.

Soon the time was almost right. Jonathan stayed closer to home and his mother and father moved into Boughey Hall to be on hand. The clock ticked by as the hours passed. Patricia was getting agitated now and feeling the discomfort. Jonathan never left her side as he waited patiently for his firstborn to make an appearance.

It was during the early hours of Sunday morning when Patricia became stressed. Mrs Godwin sat by her side whispering words of encouragement whilst Doctor John paced up and down the bedroom. Nursing staff from the infirmary had been brought in to help and Jonathan was standing close by to help his wife. Another hour passed by before the baby began to show, carefully assisted by Jonathan and his mother. Patricia was finding it difficult and would cry out. Words of encouragement came from all directions. Finally with an almighty effort, the child arrived, much to the relief of Lady Patricia who commented that it was painfully hard work giving birth and that someone should invent an easier way.

The newborn heir to Boughey Hall soon started bawling his lungs out, which raise much laughter from his parents. Jonathan held him in his arms and presented him to Patricia. "Your son is calling for you, my dear." He placed the baby in her arms; she was exhausted but radiantly happy.

Jonathan stayed with Patricia all day allowing her to rest whilst the baby was cared for by the nursing staff. Now that all the fuss was over, he would have to concentrate on his duties once more. The next day found him touring the estate on Black Bess. The farm was his first call and then the dairy; he decided to pay a visit to the disused farm that he thought would make training stable for racehorses. The river ran at the back of the farm some hundred yards away but at times the river flooded and ruined the crops, making it an impossible investment so it was abandoned. There was a large parcel of land doing nothing. Jonathan had mulled it over in his mind, if the banks of the river were raised and a large track laid down it would be ideal as a training course. The farm buildings would have to be renovated but Jonathan could see the farmhouse as living quarters for a qualified horse trainer. With the outbuilding renovated into living quarters for jockeys and the cow sheds turned into stables to house about twelve horses. Jonathan could see it turned into a viable business. He knew many noblemen kept thoroughbred horses and decided to ask around to see if any would be interested.

It was time for him to return to the house so with his mind full of ideas he made his way home. As he led Bess into the stables, he saw a saddled horse tied to the hitching rail. The saddle bore the insignia of the royal household. Lady Patricia met him in the hallway carrying their son. "You have a courier from the palace, Jonathan. He's in the drawing room." Not being able to resist a kiss for Patricia and one for the baby, he made his way to the drawing room.

Chapter 13

The courier stood up and addressed Jonathan. "Sir Jonathan, I have an urgent message from the king's secretary." He passed the satchel to Jonathan. The seal was unbroken. "Please make yourself comfortable, you have ridden a long way, I will order some refreshment for you." Jonathan moved over to the window and opened the satchel. "Sir Jonathan, I have taken it upon myself to ask if you could possibly come to the palace and see the king. His highness is ill again and is in poor shape. His doctors say he has a very bad case of diarrhoea, he never gets off the lavatory." Jonathan listened carefully, it sounded as if the king was in a bad way. "Right, we will have a quick meal and then we ride to London, over night if necessary but first I must make a quick visit to the monastery to see my friend Brother Thomas." Jonathan organised everything and then told Patricia that he would be away from home for a short while. He arranged for a fresh horse for the courier and had Bess saddled.

Brother Thomas listened carefully and shook his head. "It sounds serious, Jonathan, I'll mix up some medication for you to take with you but I'm thinking it may be a case of dysentery. We had a severe epidemic many years ago in China and it wiped out a lot of people in one village." Jonathan said he would try Brother Thomas's medication but wondered why the king's own doctors hadn't been able to help him. Brother Thomas said, "It is a matter of knowing what you are treating the patient for. The wrong diagnosis can be fatal but Jonathan, I do have a problem. A cargo ship carrying a piece of important equipment is on its way from China but the Dutch government have impounded that ship due to the problems between Holland and England, it's all political but I must have my equipment and supplies Jonathan, this particular instrument will enable me to diagnose the king's illness correctly." Jonathan didn't know what to say except, "what is the name of the ship and describe the containers and what is written on them. I'll see if the palace can come up with anything." Thomas wrote down the information. "If you get my supplies, Jonathan, I will also require you to bring a fresh sample of the king's faeces to test with my new equipment."

Jonathan and the courier rode through the night taking short rests for the horses. Very tired the two men arrived at the palace mid-morning. The king's secretary greeted Jonathan on his arrival and immediately took him to see the king. Sir Jonathan was greeted enthusiastically by his majesty who was surprised by the sudden visit. Jonathan noticed once that the king was in bad shape. A toilet on wheels had been made so as the king could move around the palace, although the stench was prolific, despite being soaked in rosewater.

"Your majesty, why haven't you sent for me sooner, you are ill, Sire." The king made some excuse about his own doctors treating him but not satisfactorily and being incompetent idiots. "Well now I am here, I want you to stay in your quarters where I can find out what is wrong with you but first, I must speak with your secretary." Lord Ashcroft greeted him again and thanked him for coming. "Let us talk in my office, Sir Jonathan, what goes on in the palace has to be kept private."

"I don't know if you can offer any help on this matter Lord Ashcroft but there is a special consignment for my friend at the monastery who is helping me but it is aboard a ship impounded in the port of Holland. This consignment included a special piece of medical equipment that Brother Thomas needs urgently and will help diagnose the king's illness, is there any way we can retrieve it?"

Lord Ashcroft rang his bell for his assistant. "I want you to find Captain Bligh for me and bring him here. He's in London somewhere, ask around and find him." The clerk left.

"Lord Ashcroft, I do appreciate your help," said Jonathan, "but now I must rest, I'm tired after riding through the night." Lord Ashcroft asked Jonathan for any information he had on the ship and the cargo. Jonathan gave him the piece of paper showing the name of the ship; the captain's name and a description of the wooden container measuring three feet by two feet by one foot and the name written on the boxes. Jonathan retired to his room and ate the food placed on the table, he then lay down and fell into a deep slumber. He awoke several hours later feeling refreshed, a quick wash and change and he made his way to the secretary's office. Lord Ashcroft beckoned him in and offered him a chair. "Good news, Sir Jonathan, we have located Captain Bligh and asked for his help. Fortunately, he tells us that he has an acquaintance who happens to be a pirate and will go anywhere at any time. All the information has been passed on to him and now we must wait. The king has been asking for you, Sir Jonathan."

His majesty looked up as Jonathan entered his room. "Ah, Sir Jonathan, I do believe you now have a young son, congratulations and I trust all is well with Lady Patricia. Lord Fairbanks writes to me occasionally and keeps me informed and I am pleased with you for taking on the responsibility of Lord Fiscal for the Staffordshire area." Jonathan sat down beside the king. "First of all, your majesty, what is your present diet consisting of?"

The king shook his head. "Nothing really, soft drinks and some soup with a mashed up chicken leg or something but within minutes, it's passed through me."

Jonathan produced the medication provided by Thomas. "Well, sire, I am going to try you on some of this medication a little at a time and see how you react to it. Your doctors say they have been giving you the normal medication for diarrhoea and it doesn't seem to be helping you, does it?"

The king shook his head. "No Jonathan and I have important decisions to make. Our problems in Havana have escalated and I need to go there as soon as I can." Jonathan informed the king that he must not travel in his condition and must be patient a little longer. He also enquired about his back problem. "It's been fine, Jonathan, thanks to you, occasionally I need to use a stick but otherwise it's fine."

Captain Bligh sent his men to search the dock areas for his unscrupulous contact Captain Baines, a notorious sea captain who ran the gauntlet across the seas for private enterprise. He was found shacked up in one of the taverns with a buxom maid. Always interested in making a few sovereigns he made his way to Captain Bligh's ship where a deal was made to sneak into the Dutch port and retrieve the consignment. That night his sloop 'The Marianne' slipped its mooring and made its way to Holland where a dense fog surrounded the coast and at least three miles out to sea. His crew consisted of eight men of dubious character and one being a China man of uncertain origin but on the run from the Chinese government. Captain Baines approached the Dutch coast but didn't enter the port. He dropped anchor two miles offshore and lowered a medium-sized rowing boat. He and four men including the China man rowed into the port and hid amongst the ships in the harbour. He and his men made fast the boat and clambered ashore. He ordered them to search for the Chinese captain amongst the dockside taverns. Two hours later, they returned with the captain of the ship 'Pride of the Orient'. Captain Baines explained their mission through the aid his Chinese crew member. A deal was made and they were led to where the boat was impounded. One guard was on board patrolling the vessel but was quickly subdued. In the hold, they searched for the boxes which were found and carried up on deck. The small rowing boat pulled alongside and the boxes were loaded onto it. The captain handed over the gold sovereigns to the Chinese captain and was soon back on board Captain Blaine's sloop. By morning, they were back in London unloading their mysterious cargo onto a cart bound for the palace. Captain Bligh showed his appreciation handing over a bag of gold coins and a case of whisky plus other items.

Lord Ashcroft entered the king's quarters and asked if Sir Jonathan could spare a few minutes. In his office, the secretary told Jonathan that the mission had been successful and the two boxes were now loaded onto two pack horses ready for Jonathan.

When Jonathan entered the king's quarters, he was carrying a glass jar. "Now sire, I have a request to make. I want you to give me a sample of your faeces next time you go to the toilet and also in this small glass a sample of your urine, we may as well do a complete test." The king looked a bit perplexed. "My doctors have never done anything like that Jonathan, what's it all for?"

The doctor told the king it was to be tested by his good friend Brother Thomas with his new equipment which he now had to deliver to the monastery post haste. "Keep taking the medication I have given you and don't move from the palace your majesty, I will return as soon as possible."

Jonathan and the courier left early next morning with the packhorse and the king's sample safely wrapped up. They made good progress, resting occasionally for food and to rest the horses. By late evening, they were crossing Cank Thorn and arrived at the monastery shortly. Brother Thomas was ecstatic at the sight of the wooden boxes and immediately opened them, revealing the piece of equipment he had been waiting for. "What is it?" asked Jonathan.

"It's a microscope," answered Thomas, "now I will examine the king's faeces and form an opinion, can you come back tomorrow, I shall be working through the night on this."

Lady Patricia welcomed Jonathan and took his hand leading him upstairs to the baby's room. Jonathan leaned over and kissed his young son whom they had decided to call Stephen. "I've missed him," whispered Jonathan, "and you too, my love."

The next morning found Jonathan pacing the floor impatiently. He was wondering what Brother Thomas had come up with. "I shall be off to London again soon," he told Patricia, "now I'm off to see what Brother Thomas has come up with." He rode across the fields to the monastery. Brother Thomas greeted him enthusiastically. "It's what I thought, Jonathan, a bad case of dysentery." Jonathan looked at the strange combination of herbs and things being boiled. "I have checked and double-checked the king's faeces. You have good and bad bacteria in your gut and the king has only bad bacteria. I have made up a combination of medicines for you to give him but first only let him drink boiled water for two days to purify his gut and then let him start on this medication gradually increasing the dosage and feeding him simple foods like soup and minced up vegetables and chicken, a little at a time. Within a week, he should show signs of improvement." Jonathan thanked him and rode back to Boughey Hall where the courier was waiting. "I'll just tell Lady Patricia and then we will ride to London again."

The king's secretary Lord Ashcroft was awaiting their arrival. Jonathan explained what was happening to the king and showed him the medicines he had brought. After a quick meal and a fresh-up, he made his way to the king's quarters. Jonathan bowed to his majesty and asked how he was. "I'm still in a poor state, Jonathan, what have you got for me?" After a brief discussion, Jonathan briefed his servants and the king was given only boiled water.

The days passed and Jonathan kept a close watch on the king's progress, gradually, he appeared to improve, especially when food was given. After a week, the king seemed a lot happier and his bowel movements improved, much to everyone's relief. The king was up and around, almost his usual self. Sir Jonathan was being treated as a hero and the secretary announced that the king was about to reward him by bestowing an Earldom on him. "It is about to be decided on your new title, Sir Jonathan, the king insists." Again Jonathan was asked to attend a ceremony in the great hall where his majesty, all pleasant and smiling, announced his appreciation and announced that Sir Jonathan Godwin Lord Fiscal to Staffordshire and the Moorlands should now be addressed as Lord Jonathan Godwin Earl of Staffordshire and the Moorlands, Lord Fiscal to the King of England. Jonathan once again thanked the king for the honour and would serve his majesty for as long as he lived.

When the ceremony was over, Jonathan paid a visit to Lord Ashcroft in his office. "I just want to say, please don't let the king go off to Havana like he intends to do. He is still delicate and should not travel. Please keep me informed of his health. I will come at once if needed." They shook hands and Jonathan made his way to the king's quarters to say he would be leaving. "Please sire, take things easy for a while. I am returning to Boughey Hall now as I am missing my family. Please send for me if you need medical attention. I am your servant, sire."

Sir Jonathan made the journey home as quick as possible, stopping only to give Bess a rest and to stretch his legs. He rode through the gates of Boughey Hall as the sun began to rise. He didn't follow the driveway, he steered Bess across the meadow to a knoll overlooking the estate. He stopped for a while looking down on scene he had witnessed many times. As the morning sunlight swept across the meadow casting shadows, he looked at the house in the distance reflecting on his dreams and aspirations that had now materialised through an accident on Etching hill. His love of Lord Fairbanks' daughter had come to fruition and now here he was beyond all his wildest dreams 'Master of Boughey Hall'.

THE END

Milton Keynes UK
Ingram Content Group UK Ltd.
UKHW022216181123
432823UK00011B/263

9 781398 462076